MW00637951

THE END BEGINS

GLIMMERING
LIGHT

A NOVEL

OTHER BOOKS AND AUDIO BOOKS
BY MARGOT HOVLEY

The End Begins: Sudden Darkness

With Wondering Awe (anthology)

THE END BEGINS

GLIMMERING LIGHT

A NOVEL

MARGOT HOVLEY

Covenant Communications, Inc.

Cover Images: *Riot in Santiago* © Luis Sandoval Mandujano, courtesy gettyimages.com
Young Couple Going through Relationship Difficulties © Aleksandar Bedov
Salt Lake Temple © Legacy Images, Inc., courtesy istockphoto.com

Cover design copyright © 2014 by Covenant Communications, Inc.

Published by Covenant Communications, Inc.
American Fork, Utah

Copyright © 2014 by Margot Hovley
All rights reserved. No part of this book may be reproduced in any format or in any medium without the
written permission of the publisher, Covenant Communications, Inc., P.O. Box 416, American Fork, UT
84003. The views expressed within this work are the sole responsibility of the author and do not necessarily reflect the position of Covenant Communications, Inc., or any other entity.

This is a work of fiction. The characters, names, incidents, places, and dialogue are either products of the
author's imagination, and are not to be construed as real, or are used fictitiously.

Printed in the United States of America
First Printing: March 2014

20 19 18 17 16 15 14   10 9 8 7 6 5 4 3 2 1

ISBN 978-1-62108-694-9

Praise for *The End Begins: Sudden Darkness*

"Hovley weaves a compelling tale of overcoming fear and finding hidden strength as a young farm girl is thrust into the midst of the unthinkable: foreign attack on the United States. My thoughts lingered on the story and its characters long after I'd read the final chapter."

—Krista Jensen

"This story never lets you take a breath; catastrophe hits and I couldn't put it down until I knew what would happen. With its subtle mix of gospel principles and nonstop action, this is a great read for young people."

—Melanie Jacobsen

"*Sudden Darkness* is an exciting adventure that will make you think about a possible future for our people—with real characters to care about, no matter your age."

—Marion Jensen

For Danny-boy,
the best test pancake

ACKNOWLEDGMENTS

THANK YOU TO THE WRITERS' Cramp: Marion Jensen, Ken Lee, Chris Miller, Christy Monson, Cory Webb, and Janette Wright. You dotted my i's and crossed my t's, but more importantly, you showed me true friendship.

Thanks to the Bear Lake Monsters: the above lovelies plus Nancy Allen, Krista Jensen, Josi Kilpack, Jenny Moore, and Robison Wells for the retreats that birthed this book. You fed me food, friendship, and the best bad guy names ever.

Other friends that helped shape this story: Hannah Porter—my wonderful source for medical info (all mistakes are mine alone), and Tami Fillmore—who gave me great insights on mother/daughter relationships, among other great things.

Thanks to my teen beta readers, especially Grace Fillmore, and to my teen writing students. You remind me that writing is a road worth walking.

Thank you to the Kaysville basketball gang. You've been there for me in so many ways. Without our morning hoops, I wouldn't be a writer. I'd hardly even be alive. Foul on.

Thank you, beautiful arrows in my quiver. Happy is the woman who hath her quiver full with such as these. Each of you, whether born to me or married in, help make my writing creations possible. Thank you, loving parents, always supportive, always encouraging. Thank you, brothers and sisters, for your patient love.

The map was created by my daughter and artist extraordinaire, Rosalie Ledezma. My author photo was taken by Erica Michaelis.

Thanks to all on the Covenant team for polishing Amélie and Zack's story to its shiny best.

Last and best, thanks to my beloved husband and favorite adventure companion, Art. Lots of people know about your mad singing skills, but I'm the only one who knows what an amazing editor you are.

There is nothing so deceptive as the distance of a light upon a pitch-dark night, and sometimes the glimmer seemed to be far away upon the horizon and sometimes it might have been within a few yards of us.

—Arthur Conan Doyle, Sr.

Get Directions

A	Salt Lake City, UT
B	Independence, MO

Get Directions

Walking directions to Independence, MO
Distance: 1084 miles, 352 hours

A Salt Lake City, UT

1. Start west on 400 South/W University Blvd towards S Main St
   33 ft

2. Turn left onto S Main St
   0.2 miles

3. Turn right onto W 500 S
   0.7 miles

4. Merge onto 1-15 S/I-80 E via the ramp to Las Vegas/Cheyenne
   2.7miles

5. Keep right to continue on I-80 E. Follow signs for Cheyenne/Interstate 80
   873 miles
   Passing through Wyoming
   Entering Nebraska

6. Take exit 397 to merge onto US-77 S/Homestead Expy towards NE-2/Beatrice/Nebraska City
   4.0 miles

7. Turn left onto Pioneer Blvd

8. Turn right onto NE-2 E
   52.4 miles
   Entering Iowa

9. Turn right onto the Interstate 29 S ramp
   0.3 miles

10. Merge onto I-29 S
    119 miles
    Entering Missouri

11. Take exit 59 to merge onto US-24 E/E Winner Rd towards Independence Ave
    4.4 miles

12. Turn right onto N Main St
    0.7 miles

13. Turn left onto E Kansas Ave

B Independence, MO

CHAPTER ONE

Amélie

I COULDN'T BELIEVE MY EYES when I read the message.

The paper felt stiff and thick between my fingers, covered with the elegant scrawl of a faceless clerk in the Church Office Building. Not an e-mail, not a sheet of computer paper lasered with words. Someone had taken up a pen and written a message.

Then they'd laid it in a messenger's hands, a messenger who then rode a bicycle to our apartment down by the old Union station on the west side of town, where he knocked on our door and asked for me. Me! Amélie Hatch, nineteen years old. Former screw-up and just a scrawny bit of nothing. Invited to a big important meeting downtown. I knew what it was about.

It had been four months since an electromagnetic pulse attack—an EMP—had taken out the US power grid, and the members of our stake—the Yakima Washington Stake—found ourselves on an unimaginable journey. We set out to *walk* to Utah. Three months later we arrived.

The very day I got to Salt Lake City, I'd been given a special assignment. Help organize the youth, they'd said. But I hadn't heard anything since then about what that meant. All the organizing I'd done was to set up my belongings in our new place. That'd taken about five minutes, since everything I owned fit in a single backpack—the one I'd carried from Washington.

I'd figured they must have made a mistake giving me that assignment. Not so hard to believe. There were probably a thousand people—or more—who'd be a better choice than me. I admit I'd felt relieved when the assignment seemed to be forgotten.

But now the courier had come with the message. My stomach lurched. So the assignment hadn't been forgotten after all. No doubt with all the people arriving—the Yakima stake wasn't the only one they pulled in—they'd had their hands pretty full. Now they could give some space to the youth project.

You can do it, I told myself. *Remember. You've done hard things before. Really hard things.*

Only a week ago, I'd done one of the very hardest things of all— even harder than walking seven hundred miles.

I said good-bye to Zack.

Every time I thought about it I got weepy and had to force myself to get tough.

A week ago, he and some other young men from our area left for Provo for their assignment with the Nauvoo Legion. Even now, I felt a physical pain, like a punch in the gut, when I thought about it.

"It's okay, Lee. We'll be back together in no time," Zack says. I stare at his face, trying to memorize every detail. His sandy-blond hair cut bristly short. His eyes with their happy crinkles. His smiling lips. I kiss them. He holds me tight, and despite his brave words, I know he feels the pain of parting too, right down to his bones. We both realize this thing between us is newborn and fragile, like a wispy seed puff tossed on a breeze, hoping to land on fertile soil and take deep root.

There were way, way too many ifs and unknowns. This wasn't like a Church mission, where a girl could count down the days until her missionary got home. I had no idea when I'd see Zack again (it better be sooner than two years!!) or what life would be like for either of us in between. We both knew war was coming. The prophet made that clear. I couldn't bear to think of the danger Zack could be heading into.

And the rest of us? We'd continue preparations to leave the Rocky Mountains for Missouri, but still, anything could happen with the government trying to regroup next door in Ogden and the rest of the country—and maybe the world—in chaos. We were isolated from what was happening outside the area, but we'd heard tidbits. The terrorists who set off the EMP were rumored to have struck an alliance with a radical government with space capability, but no one knew for sure. All we could do was guess, but we knew that in order for an EMP to have such a devastating effect, it would need to explode in the atmosphere.

Then there were the rumors of nuclear devastation on the ground, in the big cities.

At 3:00 p.m. I put on the skirt and blouse a kind girl in my new ward gave me, since I hadn't brought any dress clothes when we left Washington. After all, I could only bring one backpack.

"You look nice," Mom said. I grimaced but said nothing.

Mom wears skirts all the time—part of her weird gypsy-bohemian uniform—but I hated them. I was strictly a jeans girl except at church. That was one of the best parts about our trek—I didn't have to wear a skirt one time in two months. But for some reason, people think wearing a skirt or dress is more proper, even though, if you think about it, it doesn't make much sense. Why are legs that show (from the knee down, even) more proper than legs covered up? I guess I'm not as much of a rebel as I like to think, since I put the skirt on anyway.

The Church Office Building was maybe ten big blocks away. Before all this EMP stuff happened, I would never have considered walking that far. Not with my limp. But now, ten blocks? No big deal.

I hobbled down the apartment's steps to the sidewalk just as Dad walked up.

"Hey, you're home!" I said. "You never get home before six." Dad worked all the time at his mysterious Church job, and he always seemed to be in a rush. "Looks like they turned you loose early today."

"Hi, Lee." Dad smiled. "I came back to fetch you."

"Really? You know about this little appointment of mine?"

"Yep."

"And you walked all the way home just to turn around and walk back there with me?"

"Yep."

I didn't say so, but I felt a tingle of happiness at that. After being separated from Dad for three months during the trek from Washington, I still couldn't get enough of being around him. It'd been super hard doing it without him. Just Mom, me, Jarron, and Ethan. And, okay, two thousand of our closest friends.

He moderated his steps to match my pace. "So are you excited?"

"Uh, I guess. Should I be? Do you know what this is about?"

Dad shrugged. "Not exactly. But it'll be great for you to have something to do. You know, to keep you busy." He looked at me with that worried face he often got, the one where his eyebrows went up in the middle. I knew what he was talking about. Stuff to do to keep me from moping around. To help keep my mind off Zack.

We crossed the street, which had once been clogged with cars but was now a thoroughfare for bikers and walkers like us, along with a few horse-drawn carts rattling along beside the empty Trax rails. Down one street, men in camo marched. I couldn't see them well, but they looked armed. What were they doing?

Dad followed my eyes. His face darkened. I couldn't explain why, but I felt the need to lighten the mood.

"So what have you been working on this week?" I asked. Dad was usually pretty vague about what the Church had him doing.

"Another new agricultural project," Dad said.

Yep. Vague.

"Why the long hours?" I asked.

"Well, there's a lot going on. They've got me handling some picky little details. We have a tight schedule . . ." Vague.

At least he lived with us. We were a family again.

+

We chatted until we arrived at the Church Office Building and walked inside the spacious foyer. Light streamed through large windows, but I imagined how this space looked a few months ago, flooded with fluorescent lamps. We entered a dark stairwell beside the now-quiet elevator and climbed a few flights to the third floor. I'd heard there were twenty-eight floors, so the fact that my appointment was only on the third floor came as a relief.

We stepped into a reception area. "I'll drop you off here," Dad said. "I'll do a few things and then meet you back in the main foyer when you're finished."

"Amélie Hatch?" a woman behind the desk asked as Dad walked back to the stairs.

"Yes."

"Follow me." She led me down a hallway lit by kerosene lamps that sat on little end tables pushed up against the wall. They lent a golden flicker to an otherwise plain, corporate-looking place. She opened a door, and I followed her inside.

A man with dark, thinning hair sat behind a fine wooden desk with absolutely nothing on it but a lamp. Sunlight streamed in through a large window overlooking the city, lighting the room. I smiled to see a computer and monitor on the floor in the corner. An electronic carcass.

He rose and shook my hand. "Hello, Sister Hatch." The woman slipped out. "I'm Elder Thompson."

My heart skipped. *Elder* Thompson. That meant he was either a General Authority or a missionary. No telltale black name tag, and I felt sure I recognized him from general conference.

Me, little Amélie from Zillah, Washington. A meeting with a General Authority. I stilled a shiver and smiled.

"Hello." I forced my voice to smoothness.

"Please, sit." He waved a hand to a pair of chairs in front of the picture window.

I sat down on the edge of the tufted seat and tugged my skirt down over my knees.

He sat across from me. "You settling in okay? Getting used to Utah?"

"Uh. Yes." *Brilliant answer, Amélie*, I thought.

"The youth of the Church have so much potential." The cadence of his voice sounded just like a speaker at general conference. If he hadn't ever had that assignment, he was ready to go. Well, he had the voice part down, anyway.

He continued. "We're not going to let that go to waste in such a time. Involving them will be good for us, and it will be good for you all too. We were very impressed by the reports we received about your participation on the Yakima stake trek. We believe you're the person to be our youth liaison in this effort."

This was pretty similar to what I'd heard before, but I still swallowed hard. "What does that mean, liaison?"

"'Liaison' means you'll be the contact person, the go-between for the adult leadership and the youth. I know this sounds intimidating, but don't worry—we'll have people with leadership experience you'll report to."

"I'm good with that part," I said.

"Here's your first assignment. We need to count and compile a list of the youth in the area. Computers would do this in a snap, but since those are down, you'll need to organize teams to go out and contact the bishops. You'll gather lists of names, ages, addresses, skills, and talents. The bishops have already been assigned to create paper copies of their ward lists, so you can use that information to create a youth list. Some of the young men are already involved in the youth militia—the Nauvoo Legion. You're aware of that group?"

I nodded. Oh yes. Zack's group. I was definitely aware of them.

Like a thousand times before, my thoughts flew to Zack. I knew he'd miss me, but when we were saying our good-byes, I'd looked into his eyes. There, beside the sadness at our separation, I saw the fire of adventure. *I'll miss you more*, I thought. *Go be the brave soldier, but you better not get hurt, Zack Allman.* He wasn't the kind to take foolish chances, but he'd already proven he liked to play the hero.

He'd risked his life to rescue me from the fake cops in the Pendleton Pen. He'd ended up jumping in front of a bullet, and it had taken a flat-out miracle for him to recover from that. I shuddered at the memory of him lying there in the doctor's tent, still and pale as a corpse. I'd never been so scared, no, not even when my kidnappers had thrown a burlap sack over my head and carted me off.

I had no idea what lay in store for him in the Nauvoo Legion. Would he have to really fight? How soon? If I allowed myself, I could end up sick with worry.

So I wouldn't allow it. I forced myself to listen as Elder Thompson gave me more details.

—|—

Down the stairs I went, my head spinning. Elder Thompson's instructions cascaded through my mind like a torrent. He'd finished by saying this was only the first assignment of many.

While we walked home, Dad got me started working out my new task, helping me make a plan for systematically creating a list of the young people. I clutched both the precious handwritten list of bishops and their respective stakes and a letter of introduction that Elder Thompson had given me as I left his office. I'd need a lot of help— obviously a committee of sorts—exactly the kind of thing that terrified me. I'd much rather tramp around Utah for months and do it all myself than to ask people to help me and to boss them around.

We walked past a shuttered bakery. I thought about how nice it would be to step inside, smell all that carb deliciousness, and pick something up to take home. Maybe rolls to surprise Mom or doughnuts for the boys. But of course, the bakery hadn't been operational since the EMP. Sure, they could probably get the ovens converted somehow, but how would they sell their wares? No one used money anymore. Without the government behind it, dollar bills were just worthless pieces of paper. Everything was on the barter system, and even after a month to get used to it, it still was really weird. Dad worked for the Church now, but instead of a paycheck he earned food and other items from the Church storehouses. It was interesting to see the things that had become commodities—almost like money. Jewelry. Tools. Bullets.

We walked up the steps to our apartment. "I've been thinking about how you can really get this project rolling," Dad said. "What you need is a crew of strong young men on bikes."

"Yeah, like all the guys that got snatched up for the Nauvoo Legion," I grumped.

"Now, Lee-lee, open your mind to other possibilities. I mean, look at your brothers. They're too young to be in the Legion, but they're part of the group that's to be counted—the twelve to eighteens, right? So why not use them and others their age to be your legs?"

"Hmm," I said. "Not a bad idea."

"Bikes can actually cover good distances," Dad said. "After all, even before the EMP, they used them for couriers in big cities because they could get around traffic. Now it's even more of a good idea."

I spent the evening sketching ideas for dividing the Valley into areas and trying to figure out how to deploy helpers. Some willing people, like my brothers, didn't have bikes. Maybe others had bikes to lend. Somehow I'd need to match them up, puzzle out a way to recruit more, and then send them out with surveys.

I drew up the survey, which was quite simple: name, address, age, interests, and skills. I hoped people would be cool about it and not hide their skills like people hid the fact they played the piano from the seminary teacher.

The next morning, a Saturday, I decided to do a test run on my own ward. I thought I might as well see if any problems came up before I started sending out helpers. Utah wards seemed to be ridiculously small in square miles, so hopefully it wouldn't be so bad in terms of walking distance.

I went to the bishop's house, armed with notebook and pen. Luckily, I caught him at home. Once I showed him the letter Elder Thompson had given me to verify I was under the Church's direction, he willingly recited the names of the young people in his boundaries. I'd met most of them at church.

I went back by our place and wheedled Ethan and Jarron to come with me—for moral support more than anything else.

"Come on, guys. Think of it as an excuse to say hi to some cute girls."

They both tried to pretend that was stupid, but little flushes of pink on their cheeks told me otherwise.

One of the girls on the list lived right across the hall of our apartment complex, a seventeen-year-old named Cherilynn. I knocked on her door, tapping my foot in nervous anticipation. I hoped people would be willing to help or maybe even be excited. But what if they thought it was weird? Or what if the fact that I was the one presenting it put them off?

Cherilynn came to the door.

"Uh, hi." I gulped.

Cherilynn smiled at me and gave Ethan and Jarron a quizzical but friendly grin. "Hi. You're A—Am—. Sorry, I'm about to slaughter your name."

"Ah-may-lee," I said, smiling big to show I didn't mind. "You can call me Lee if you want."

"Okay, Lee, what's up?"

"The Church has asked me to do a survey of the youth . . . interests, talents, stuff like that." I wiggled my clipboard.

"What for?"

"I think they are hoping they can tap into us for help, you know, with the big trek coming up and all."

"Hey, good idea. They ought to put us to work. There has to be a pile of young people around here, right?" She stepped outside and waved at the stairs. "How about we sit here?" We each took a step to sit on.

"All right, so tell me a little about what you're interested in," I said.

"Well, I used to be way into sports—the school basketball team—volleyball too. But I haven't gotten to play much at all since everything happened. No school, you know. But you don't have to write that down. The Church wouldn't care about that kind of thing."

"No, they do. They'd like to know anything you want to say. You never know how the info might be useful." I scribbled *sports* on the clipboard with only a tiny twinge of jealousy at the sight of her long, healthy legs.

"What else?"

"Hmm. Well, I used to help out at my dad's office once in a while, with filing and stuff. Sometimes I did some computer work—entering inventory or bills if they got behind. But once again, not too useful, I'd say. Dad hasn't been able to operate his business at all since spring. It was a software company."

I wrote *office skills.*

"I can't really think of anything else," Cherilynn said. "I feel pretty useless."

"What did you do for your Personal Progress projects?" I prompted.

Her face lit up. "I made a quilt for my room, and I got my green belt in karate."

I wrote *sewing* and *karate.*

"Do you by chance have a bicycle?" I asked.

"Yeah, sure. But I really like riding my skateboard better."

"Great, great," I said, noting that. "One more question and then we're done. You're right about there being a ton of young people. How would you like to help with the survey project? I could really use you and anyone else who wants to. As many as I can get."

"What would I have to do?"

"You could help us go through the rest of our ward, doing surveys just like we did with you. Or what I could really use is someone who could help me go out and find helpers in each stake." I held my breath. What would she say? I tried to remind myself that she was just one person, and if she said no, it didn't mean everyone I asked would turn me down. It didn't mean I was dumb or doing it wrong. *Stupid negative thoughts! Get outta here.*

She shrugged. "Okay, I guess I could do that. I want to help the Church if I can."

"Yay!" I tried not to gush. I told her my ideas for contacting the stakes to find a handful of surveyors each—hopefully at least one per ward. She actually sounded excited and said she'd start copying out my little survey form to be handed to our new recruits.

Copy machines? Those used to be nice.

When we left, Jarron and Ethan each took a form. We split up and contacted most of the rest of the kids in the ward. Not everyone was as easy to talk to as Cherilynn—some just said, "I can't do anything," no matter how I prompted them. But overall, I felt good about it. Maybe this was going to work after all. Maybe I could make a difference.

And then it started to really sink in that I'd need an entire army of people like Cherilynn to cover the huge area included in the Wasatch Front. The sheer enormity of the task started to overwhelm me.

Don't choke, Amélie, I told myself. *Cowboy up. God might be busy planning the end of the world, but He can still help you.*

CHAPTER TWO

Zack

I THRUST MY ARMS INTO the sleeves of my new uniform, feeling the heavy cotton cloth slide across my skin. I buttoned the brass buttons down the front and paused a moment, my fingers tracing the small, neat stitches of the jacket pocket. Amazing.

Someone sewed this uniform by hand, with a needle and thread. The time that must have taken—for this uniform and 2,059 others.

2,060. The number of young men in the newly formed Nauvoo Legion. I got the reference right away—the same number as in Helaman's stripling army. Even though I was a brand-new Mormon, I caught that, since the story had stood out like someone shouted it that first time I read the Book of Mormon. I'd already noticed when Mormons heard the words *stripling warriors*, they got a faraway gleam in their eyes. Sort of pride and yearning all rolled up together. That army seemed to have had an almost magical protection. I had to admit, I didn't mind if we got us some of that ourselves.

I put on my old boots. They were nicely broken in after walking all the way to Utah. I guess you could say I was broken in pretty well too. The uniform (they'd wanted navy blue like the original Legion but could only find khaki cloth in bulk) would include boots at some point, but apparently, they were even harder to make by hand than the clothing. So no boots yet. No big deal.

The last bit was buckling on the holster for my handgun, the same one I'd brought from Zillah. The same one I'd killed a man with. In my mind, God had forgiven me, but the memory still chilled me. Forgiving myself was a tough deal.

We bunked at the MTC in Provo since there weren't missionaries there anymore. That sort of thing was on hold. Maybe forever.

The guys I'd met so far were mostly from Utah, but there were a few out-of-staters like me. The only soldier I knew from back home was that singer, Ryan Cook. I got to know him on the Zillah–to–Salt Lake City journey, but it's not like we were best friends or anything. He knew Amelie pretty well though. Probably because he was always hitting on her.

But that doesn't matter anymore, I told myself. *She's my girl now*. Or as much as she could be with us not living near each other.

I gave a begrudging thought to how stinking easy it used to be to call or text or walk across the gravel road that separated our farms when I wanted to talk to her. We'd grown up together, and I got used to having her around all the time. But that was then, before all the stuff happened. Now, although we were both in Utah, she was forty miles away. It might as well have been a thousand.

I really hated leaving her. I knew I had a duty to perform, and I wouldn't shirk it. But that didn't make it any easier. She'd hate me saying so, but she needed looking after, and it killed me that I couldn't do that right now. I thought about the endless number of men who'd had to leave loved ones in the past to go to war. How did they do it?

Was that me now? Was I going to war?

So much had changed. If you got right down to it, there was pretty much nothing about my life that was the same as one year ago.

Getting baptized? Huge. I never saw that coming. Falling in love with my best friend? I have to admit, that one I'd always hoped for. Trading farming for soldiering? Wow.

And of course, the whole world was different—no electricity, no real communication, no actual government. All those changes in only one year? How about four months.

We'd been divided into fifty-man companies with a captain over each. In the three days we'd been there, we'd done mostly drills and cleaning and whatnot. We went out for a little target practice, though not much because there wasn't a lot of ammo to spare. Lots of guys had never even fired a gun before, and I could tell they were freaking out a little. I didn't see anyone else with their own gun.

That ammo had to be saved for the big unknown thing we'd been called together to do. I never stopped wondering exactly what that was.

My company filed into a courtyard between a classroom building and the gym, and then Captain Christensen called us to order. "Men, we have a special assignment."

So it begins, I thought. I felt a prickle of fear. My fingers strayed over the gun holstered at my side—my thoughts flickering back to that day, that terrible day. My father's body, his blood leaching into the gravel driveway. My hand raising the pistol. The truck's back window shattering. More blood, more death. I shuddered.

That experience brought me lower than I'd ever been. Was I prepared to fire at a human being again? I swallowed hard. I thought of another time when I was the one being shot. Not awesome, although it'd led to a straight-up miracle.

I waited, feeling like I stood on a precipice.

"We're marching over to BYU," Captain Christensen said. "Just a few minutes away." Nervous under-the-breath laughs filtered from the group. BYU? Even I knew that wasn't where the bad guys were.

Captain Christensen smiled. He wasn't all gung-ho about military precision, so a little laughter didn't bug him much. "It may not sound like it, but this is actually a very important assignment, and yes, you need to keep it to yourselves. The boys over at BYU have been busy. They're building some special equipment—special enough that it needs an escort. We're taking it under our wing all the way to the new HQ."

The new HQ. Missouri. We glanced at each other with eyes full of questions.

"The details are on a need-to-know basis, but here are the essentials: We're escorting a wagon train of sorts. Along with the special cargo, there are other supplies that we'll be taking along, sort of as decoys. All the cargo will be loaded on horse-drawn wagons, with the important things hidden in with the supplies. We'll form its guard."

Okay then! I thought. This sounded awesome. Important. Secretive. Maybe not majorly dangerous.

"Grab your duffles and meet back in ten. We'll march over and help assemble the wagons, which are already there waiting. Then we take off."

A tall, beefy guy with shaggy blond hair and freckles raised a hand. "Sir, we'll be traveling on foot, then? Alongside the wagons?"

"Nope. Horseback. The command is allocating horses for each of us. This ought to tell you how important this assignment is and how swiftly we need to see it done. Dismissed."

I thought about the questions they'd asked about my background when they set up the companies. The questions had seemed random, but now they started making sense. Like "How much experience have you had with horses?" or "Have you ever driven a team before?" I looked at the other guys, and I realized most of them had that country-boy look.

So. We were a cavalry unit.

Awesome.

─┼─

We marched to BYU, if you could call it marching. We didn't step in rhythm or anything—just walked in a somewhat-orderly group.

I looked at the other guys as I walked. Many of them talked and laughed with each other as they went—obviously, some of them were friends who'd joined the Legion together. Even though they surrounded me, I felt isolated. I knew the guys in my company a little, but they weren't much more than names and faces so far. I assumed most of them had been members all their lives. I had to be one of the newest, with my baptism only two months ago. I knew it was wrong to think of myself as second class, but it was hard not to. There was so much to being a Mormon I didn't get yet. Sometimes it sounded like they were talking in secret code.

The campus looked beautiful, though maybe a little bedraggled compared to what it probably once was. There wasn't time or resources to send out swarms of gardeners to trim and weed and fuss anymore. Still, I admired the trees shading us as we made our way between the buildings.

And then there were those incredible mountains forming the backdrop, blotting out the sky with their massiveness. I still wasn't used to the mountains, even after seeing them every day since I got here. They leapt out of the ground to a ridiculous height. Huge. I wasn't sure what the big "Y" on the mountainside meant. Obviously something to do with BYU, but what? I'd never seen anything like that before coming to Utah. Was it a Mormon thing?

We walked to a parking lot on the southwest end, and I couldn't help grinning. Instead of cars, the lot held five wagons and a whole bunch of horses in a makeshift corral. I felt chills of anticipation. I'd grown up riding, and it was one of the things I missed the most about my home in Zillah.

One of those horses would be mine.

The wagons looked different than I expected. Why I thought they'd be like a pioneer covered wagon, I didn't know. These looked light, with thin wood planks forming the sides about three feet tall from bed to top and maybe ten feet long.

Men were hitching teams to the wagons as we walked up. I looked at the rigging with curiosity. I'd heard of four-in-hand rigging, allowing one man to hold the reins of four horses at once, but I'd never seen it close up. I wondered if that was as tricky as it sounded.

Captain Christensen pulled a paper from his pocket and unfolded it. "Okay, listen up. Report to the men at the corral—they'll help you find a mount. Then take it to the tack area and saddle up."

I hurried over to the men standing at the opening to the corral, which had been made by rolling dead vehicles into lines to form an area about forty feet square. Kinda funny that now, the late model Hondas or BMWs we used to admire were pretty much worthless—except for weird tasks like keeping horses from running off. An old piece-of-junk truck was a hundred times more valuable since it would actually still run.

As I approached, my eye caught a fine-looking, rust-colored gelding with white "socks." A man held the horse's lead rope. He watched as I neared, eying me closely. Finally, he spoke. "His name's Socks. He doesn't have a fancy bloodline, but he's got a good heart. He'll be a good horse—if you can handle him."

It sounded like a challenge. "Well, maybe he and I have something in common then."

The answer seemed to satisfy him. "Have fun." He handed over the lead rope, and I slipped past him into the corral, walking slowly toward the horse, which eyed me cautiously.

"Hey, boy," I said softly, holding out the lead rope as I approached. "See this?" Socks whickered and backed away from me, bunching in with some other horses. But I kept up a quiet stream of words, mostly nonsense, and moved nice and slow. It looked like he was debating whether or not to trust me. I caught hold of his halter just as he was about to break from the group. I clipped on the lead. He pranced and pulled back on the rope, but I held it firm. I sensed his energy. I knew horses fairly well, and this one wanted to run.

I stroked his strong, glossy neck. "Pretty boy. That's it. Good boy. You and I are going to spend some time together." I led him away from the other horses toward the corral opening. He tossed his head against the lead and frisked, but he soon came along well enough. Behind the corral, I saw large piles of tack—brushes, pads, saddles, and bridles—and after tying the lead to a car's side mirror, I soon had Socks ready to go.

A guy from Santaquin named Christian stood beside me with his mount. While the rest of our company got situated with horses, we watched as others stacked the wagons with crates, sacks, and barrels. Some obviously contained food for man and beast. Others I couldn't tell.

"I wonder what the mysterious cargo is," Christian said, taking off his cowboy hat to rub a hand through shaggy ginger curls. "Hidden among the regular stuff, huh? I wonder if they've got it down in the bottom of a grain barrel, like Joseph Smith and the gold plates."

"Uh, yeah." I smiled and nodded even though I didn't have a clue what he was talking about. Joseph Smith hid his gold plates in a grain barrel? Okay.

When they finished loading, other men climbed onto the wagon seats, one on each wagon. They started maneuvering the wagons out into the street, and I watched in admiration as they skillfully directed their teams. I itched to climb into my saddle and see how Socks and I would get along, but no one was mounting yet.

"There's one more thing for you boys," Captain Christensen pointed to some long, open boxes to the side of the tack piles. "Each of you take one of these and buckle it to your saddle. Grab a pouch of ammo too."

I stepped up to the boxes and looked inside. There sat fifty rifles in leather scabbards of all sizes and shapes. I grinned and pulled out a nice thirty-ought-six.

Now we're talking.

CHAPTER THREE

Amélie

SUNDAY WAS OUR FIRST STAKE conference since we arrived in Utah. I sat in the back of the stake center's gym with Mom, Dad, and the boys. I discovered one stake center looks much like another. The folding chairs felt just like the ones in the Yakima stake center—hard and sort of tippy. One big difference: it was dark. Gas lamps lit the stand and most of the chapel, but the gym was quite dark.

I glanced sidelong at my parents as we sang the opening hymn, "If You Could Hie to Kolob." Dad looked tired, barely mumbling the words. Mom warbled in her typical Carole King voice, leaning forward earnestly, looking up at the illuminated chorister far away in the front of the room. Because you're supposed to. Endearing but somehow annoying. I asked myself why I felt that way.

Mom. Sometimes her endlessly cheerful way of putting her shoulder to the wheel wore on me, tired me out. Maybe it was because she made me feel guilty. I put my shoulder to the wheel with the best of them, but I wasn't always cheery about it.

My eyes traveled to Jarron and Ethan. Stake conference used to be an endurance contest with those two a mass of wiggles, bits of paper, and crushed Cheerios. Two hours that seemed like forever. Now they were thirteen and fifteen—too old for a continuous poking contest. Scrunched down in their chairs, they seemed to consist of mostly long legs and big feet. Still, when Ethan caught me looking at him, he winked and gave me his best mischief-maker grin.

The hymn ended, and in typical Mormon-meeting fashion, a sister was immediately front and center to say the opening prayer. That was the last typical thing about this meeting.

President Carroll approached the low pulpit. Without power, it couldn't move, and the microphone didn't work either. He used a megaphone that actually worked pretty well, although it was weird to look at the speaker with that thing in front of his face.

"Brothers and sisters, thank you for your faithfulness. We in the stake presidency are consistently impressed by your dedication and obedience, and we appreciate the chance to serve you. Now I must ask for more. I have a special message for you from the prophet. You know we've been preparing for some time for our eventual gathering to Missouri. The prophet has given us the word, through our area authority, that we are to move that date forward. As a matter of fact, he has asked us to prepare to leave as quickly as we possibly can."

A buzz of shocked whispers swept the room.

A thousand questions zoomed through my mind. I whispered to Dad, "I thought this would be done slowly. The Church was going to help the government get reestablished in Ogden."

Dad opened his mouth but fell silent as President Carroll continued.

"There are a couple of reasons. It seems the government—if you can call it that—isn't satisfied with Ogden. It wants Salt Lake too. It's confiscating our buildings and the supplies we haven't moved east yet."

"They're kicking us out?" I hissed. *Like in the old days,* I thought, *except backward.*

"We can't allow our stores to be taken, but perhaps that alone wouldn't cause such drastic action if the prophet didn't feel we should move now. Many will ask, are we not to be subject to kings, presidents, and rulers, as our Articles of Faith say? The answer is yes. But the country isn't in one piece anymore. Different groups control different sections. The one that's here in Ogden is only one faction. And just so you know, the people you may have known in our state government or at Hill Air Force Base are not the ones who control this faction. Little is known about who they really are. I'm sorry to say that what once was the United States is covered in conflict—conflict between the factions and from outside the U.S. as well."

Whoa. The U.S. *covered* in war?

I knew terrorists had attacked; the government wasn't functioning, but life in Salt Lake City seemed calm, almost normal. The idea that the rest of the country was in turmoil made troubles seem all the more real.

"Another reason is that many refugees from other areas are flowing into the Wasatch Front in search of food and shelter. To help relieve some of the pressure, we're sending a large group on to Missouri where the Church has large food stores in place in preparation for our great gathering there. Be aware that although the Church has a few vehicles, they will be carrying mostly gasoline and water. This means those of you who choose to be part of this vanguard group will need to transport your own belongings and food. For most of us, this means handcarts."

Handcarts. I had to be dreaming.

"No one will be forced to leave. Many people will choose to stay. But a legitimate danger has arisen, causing the prophet to move up the timetable. So yes, there will be many thousands of people involved. We're estimating about one-third of the LDS population in this area will choose to go. Interestingly, there's a prophecy about how many will be in that first group—around two hundred thousand. And that's pretty much what we estimate the numbers will look like."

Two hundred thousand! What would a group that size be like? A hundred times bigger than our trek from Washington!

"Here are our next steps: Prayerfully decide if you'll join us. The bishops will be contacting each of you to get your decision and give you assignments. In the meantime, gather your food storage and camping equipment. Think about how to stay warm. We'll leave September 1, and we're going to be living out of doors for the next three months, at least. Saying that it's going to be cold is, well, an understatement.

"The obvious question is, why leave now? Why not wait until spring, since traveling at this time of year will be so difficult, so dangerous? The prophet has received a warning that we must pay attention to. The people who are trying to structure a government in Ogden have developed a dangerous technology, in spite of our current lack of electricity. They are looking to control the population, and their first step will be to inject a tracking device into each person. They say this is for national security, but in reality, it is a matter of agency. They have been working on this for some months and are ready to begin. This tracking device will be required in order to buy or sell. It won't be optional. The prophet feels this threat to your agency is sufficient to decide to leave now. He also feels that if we wait, it will only be harder to leave as chaos grows and these factions wield more and more power.

"One more announcement, and then I'll let you go to your preparations. Many of you already have your missionary family members back with you and the rest are attempting to return home as soon as possible. As of now, the Church has discontinued all formal missions. Of course, we should always share the gospel whenever we can, but formal missions for both the young and the senior couples are discontinued. By the way, this is also according to prophecy. As Brigham Young said, the Lord will now teach His own lessons through earthquake, flood, and famine."

I'm sure there was a closing prayer, though I didn't hear it. I stumbled out of the stake center with the rest, numb with shock. As we crossed the parking lot, I felt a hand on my shoulder.

"Sister Hatch?"

I turned to see the first counselor in our stake presidency, President Casey.

"Uh, hello."

"I have a message for you from Elder Thompson. He spoke with you earlier about a special assignment as a youth liaison, correct?"

"Yes."

"He wanted you to know that in spite of the new timetable, he'd still like you to work on the youth census project during our journey— that is, if you choose to come. What do you think? Of course, you don't have to decide this moment."

I stared back at him. I thought about what it would be like to stay. To keep living in our little apartment—maybe get a job or even go to school if such a thing became possible again. To not walk another endlessly long highway. My leg throbbed just thinking about it.

I hesitated only a moment before I smiled at President Casey. "What a question. Of course I'm going. Sign me up."

+

We walked home, Mom's arm hooked through mine, talking quietly about the stunning twenty-minute stake conference. I shook my head. I ought to be used to weird stuff by now.

Jarron and Ethan seemed cheerful enough with their happy-go-lucky "whatever" attitudes. I found myself feeling bad for them—they'd miss the usual things kids their age had taken for granted—city league soccer, Facebook, movie nights. Then again, they were skipping the torture of junior high. Maybe it was a wash.

Of course, they'd miss those things whether or not they went on this new trek. There was still no expected date for power to be restored.

It didn't surprise me that the family didn't even discuss whether we'd go. We knew without saying that we'd be a part of the group. An easy decision.

We walked into the parking lot of our apartment building—mostly empty except for the Bluebird, our old beater truck—so old that it was one of the few vehicles not affected by the EMP. The stake had borrowed it for our trek, using the precious gas they'd gathered. The Church returned it to us when we arrived in Salt Lake City, and we'd parked it here. They'd asked us to keep it available, and they'd used it a few times to haul things, but we hadn't driven it ourselves. Gas was far too valuable, and where would we get more even if we wanted to?

Around the Bluebird stood five men in combat dress with scary-looking guns slung across their backs. One look and I knew what those men were here for. The Bluebird—and not to "borrow" like the Church had done. The truck I'd grown up with, riding in its bed to and from our fields, pulling our pop-up camper on road trips, driving to high school. The truck we climbed in to leave our home in Zillah and start our long trek to Utah.

The truck I fell under as a kid, crushing my leg.

We had either awesome or terrible timing, depending on how I looked at it. If we hadn't walked up just then, no doubt they'd have taken the truck without so much as a word.

"What are you doing?" Dad demanded in his tough, no-nonsense voice.

"We're here to appropriate this vehicle. Government orders," one of the soldiers said.

"For what reason?"

"The government requires any vehicle old enough to be operational to be surrendered to central command. All such vehicles are needed to facilitate the reestablishment of the government."

Mom leaned over and whispered something in Ethan's ear. He quietly backed away from the group and disappeared around the corner of the apartment building. Mom put her arm around my shoulder and tried to draw me away, but I planted my Chuck Taylors (yes, I wore them to church) and held my ground.

"For all I know, you're just a bunch of guys wearing camo. Why should I give you my truck?" Dad asked.

"See this?" The soldier put his right hand to his temple in a saluting motion. There near his temple was a tattoo—a star within a circle. His stiff fingers pointed right to it. "The military is using this mark now. You can trust that those with this mark are from the government."

I stared. A mark on his forehead, though to the side. Could that be "the mark of the beast" I'd heard about so often in Sunday School and seminary? I felt a shiver of fear. I'd thought the mark was supposed to be something you had to have to buy or sell rather than a military thing. And this didn't appear to be the same thing the stake president had talked about—an implanted chip. This looked to be just on the skin.

I knew one thing. Just looking at it creeped me out.

At that moment, I heard a lot of other voices—men's voices—followed by the distinctive *click-ching* of rifle chambers being loaded.

Nine men surrounded the Bluebird, holding rifles trained on the army guys. Most of them wore church clothes—no doubt newly arrived home from stake conference, just like us. The soldiers started to reach for the weapons across their shoulders.

"Don't move toward your weapons. Slowly step away from the truck," one of the new men said. I recognized him as Pete Webb from our Salt Lake ward.

"Look," the soldier said, "this is government business. Back off."

"What government are you talking about?"

"The United States of America."

Pete laughed. "Are you talking about that bunch hanging out at Hill Air Force Base? You aren't any government I recognize, and you aren't taking this truck."

"I don't recommend you put yourself at odds with the state. You'll regret it," the soldier said. "Order will be restored. People who don't cooperate will find themselves sorry."

"And I recommend you take your sorry selves off," Pete retorted.

Everyone stood still in a massive stare-down. I guessed the soldier didn't like the odds and motioned his men to follow him out of the parking lot.

"Your lack of cooperation has been noted. We'll be back," he said, face red with fury. They marched off.

Dad turned to the ward men. "Thanks."

"We've had reports of fuel confiscations all over the city, including seizing wherever they find it. They say there's not a drop of gas left to be had. But we're not going to let them just take our stuff."

Another man joined in. "I believe the Church planned to help out with getting the government resettled—until government officials started being a bit too greedy. They're trying to take the Church's commodities. All of them. And you know, between the welfare system and the massive food stores, there's a lot. Oh, and they want the buildings downtown. Now all the vehicles that run."

Dad nodded. "So I've heard. No doubt one of the main reasons we're taking off. "

I looked at the men leaning on rifle stocks. "So we're not going to fight?"

Pete smiled grimly. "Oh, there will be fighting. Don't think they're going to just let us walk away with all the stuff. But since we're supposed to end up in Missouri anyway, it's better to leave now. Plus, there's that whole thing about them planning to force that nanobot ID thing on everyone. Not okay."

"At least there will be less interference from this so-called government once we get to Missouri," Mom said in my ear as she led me back to our apartment. "You're going to like it there."

"I'm not going to like walking there." It was over a thousand miles to Missouri, compared to seven hundred on our trek from Washington State.

I thought back to when we left Zillah, leaving behind everything except a change of clothes. All our comforts and belongings. Keepsakes, books, photos. My piano. My favorite gadgets, although none of them worked anymore.

"There will be a way," Mom said.

I'd already decided I'd be right there at the front when the word came to go, but still, it stung. The Mormons, getting kicked out of their beautiful city. Again.

I knew it wasn't the same. No one was holding a torch to our homes or throwing us out into a blizzard. But still, the thought rankled. What about the Tabernacle? What about the temple? What would happen to the things we couldn't bring with us?

"What if they chase us?" I asked, my voice nearly a whisper.

"Well, they probably will." Mom pulled me into a hug. I let her. She was being weirdly strong, I thought. I considered collapsing on her and crying about all my frustrations and fears, but that had never been my way. As usual, I bottled that stuff inside and forced it down.

I bit my bottom lip. My thoughts flew to Zack, preparing for his duties with the Nauvoo Legion. What kind of danger did this put him in? I shivered.

I didn't let myself think about the other worry that crouched like a shadow in my mind. Me, walking another ridiculously long road, falling behind, hurting, stumbling. Being a burden. I tried to picture myself pulling a handcart. What a joke.

I couldn't decide if I was more angry or scared.

CHAPTER FOUR

Zack

WE SET OUT, FUNNELING THROUGH Provo to the highway leading up the canyon. The wagons took the middle of the road, but we mostly stuck to the shoulder and side areas to protect the horses' feet. The horses pulling the wagons had special "boots" on their hooves—the removable kind. Walking on asphalt wasn't great for a horse, especially for long distances. I noticed that the horses who weren't wearing boots were unshod. I nodded to myself. Dad always said keeping a horse barefoot was best for traction.

There were five wagons, so it worked out to about ten of us per. For the most part, we bunched loosely around the wagons but took turns riding out front and back to keep watch.

Socks loved it when it was our turn to scout. He got antsy trying to keep the steady pace of the wagons. We passed through some pretty country, the road angling upward into the trees and rocky bluffs. Acres of aspens bordered the highway. I didn't see a single soul as Socks huffed his way up, up, up. I saw a few pointed rooftops within the trees—apparently cabins—but not much evidence of people.

After two hours, we halted to water and feed the horses. For now, we had the Provo River handy, but we carried empty barrels for water in one of the wagons for when water was scarce. Socks was warm but not too winded. When we dismounted, I saw that quite a few guys looked sore. I wasn't going to say so, but I felt it myself. After all, I hadn't ridden a horse in months.

Just wait till tomorrow, guys, I thought. *If you think you're stiff now . . .*

We continued on, stopping to let the horses graze every hour or so, ending up with about eighteen miles the first day. The captain gave the signal to halt at Deer Creek State Park.

"Eighteen miles," I said to Christian as we rode into the parking lot. "That would have taken us, what, twenty minutes to drive?"

"Ugh," Christian groaned, sliding out of the saddle and looping his reins around a tree branch. Our horses fell happily to cropping grass while we pulled off their tack and brushed them down. "I'm used to working on horseback, but it ain't a great way to go anywhere fast."

Once everyone had finished brushing down their horses, the captain had Christian show us how to tie hobbles on our mounts—allowing them to move around enough to graze to their liking but not enough to take off. In spite of having had horses on our farm for years, I'd never used hobbles before.

We prepared to camp outside instead of inside a church like we'd done so often on Trek #1. With only fifty-five, counting the wagon-masters, space wasn't an issue. Plus, it was plenty nice out—not cold at all. On Trek #1, there were lots of women and children with us, and having a roof over their heads was nice for them. But our current group was all men.

I grinned to myself. I stopped thinking of myself as a boy long ago, but calling myself a man seemed a bit more legit now.

After a supper of dutch oven chicken and bread, we sacked out. That part seemed almost normal to me after doing it so often on Trek #1. The other guys looked like it was no big deal for them either. I'd heard Mormons were huge on scouting, so I guessed they'd been camping a bunch before.

In the morning, we limped around getting ready—men, perhaps, but more like old, arthritic men. My thighs throbbed, and there were chafed places I didn't want to even acknowledge. Still, I wasn't the worst off by a long shot. I saw guys who looked like they were about to cry when they pulled themselves back into their saddles.

As we rode along the deserted highway, my eyes roamed the hills. My view was pretty unobstructed, and I found it hard to imagine anyone swooping down on us without being noticed. Maybe one of our biggest challenges would be trying to keep from being too complacent. Zero chance of me falling asleep in the saddle though. My legs hurt way too much. Still, my mind raced, thinking about what we might face farther on.

I managed to sidle Socks up next to the captain. I had questions on my mind. "Captain, just wondering . . . I know we're here to guard these . . . items, and make sure they get to Missouri safely. You had us train and practice a few things in Provo, but there wasn't much time. We sort of don't know what to do. Are we expecting someone to attack us and try to take the stuff? If they do, what exactly are we supposed to do? Fire at them? Seems like we should maybe go through some scenarios or something."

The captain smiled and reached over to clap me on the shoulder. "You're right, son, and you'll see very soon what we're going to do about that. I'll be addressing that very issue when we stop for the night." He clucked his tongue at his horse and trotted ahead to take his turn at scouting.

I watched him get smaller and smaller as he moved away. Okay. Tonight we'd make plans.

We camped that night at Jordanelle State Park along the shores of Jordanelle Reservoir. We got the horses settled and topped off their water barrels in the reservoir. There were plenty of picnic areas and fire pits so we put those to use for supper.

Afterward, the captain gathered us together, the wagonmasters standing near him. Most of us sat on or around picnic tables; the rest lounged on the sandy ground. I heard plenty of groans from guys about their sore legs as the captain got started.

"Men, good job on making it through your first two days without much trouble. Just a few more days, and your bodies should be used to all this riding. Hang in there." Rueful chuckles and a few outright grumbles rippled through the group.

"As you know we have a long way to go, and our mission is of the utmost importance. We wanted to get underway before we put our plan into place, but here's what we're going to do. Tomorrow, noonish, we'll get to the turnoff. The road tees—one way goes toward our Missouri destination, and the other heads back toward Salt Lake. We're going to split the group up. Most will stay with the main group and wagons, but we're going to break off two little teams of three men each. One team will head to Salt Lake City, deliver some messages, and then join the rest of the Legion heading to Missouri. The other team will head for Missouri but on a separate route, which I'll go over with the people involved. Both small teams are going to function as a diversion of sorts. Decoys. Outsiders won't know where the actual cargo is. As a matter of fact, the teams themselves may not even know for sure."

A buzz of amazement spread through the group. I held my breath. More. I needed more information.

"Our mission is already being watched. The people working against us are aware we're on the move. They aren't just thinking about stopping us; they *will* try." The captain took a deep breath, pulled a paper from his pocket, and unfolded it. "Now, then. I'll tell you which people are going where."

My mind swirled. Which group would I be put in? Which group did I want to be in? Salt Lake City—the thought made my heart lurch. Amélie. She was there. If I went with that group, I'd most likely get a chance to see her. I probably wouldn't be able to travel with her like last time, but I might be able to help her out. It felt like forever since we'd been together, even though it had been less than a month. The thought became almost overwhelming. I stared at the captain, almost willing him to read my name out for that team.

"For the Salt Lake team: Matthew Miller, Chris Lee, and Ken Buckley." I bit my lip, forcing myself to swallow my disappointment. I looked around to find the chosen men. At first I was surprised to see they looked sort of down about it, but I asked myself—*if Amélie wasn't in Salt Lake City, would I really want to go that way?* I'd probably choose to stay with the main cavalry group, if the choice was up to me. Surely that's where the "critical" items would stay. Surely that's where the most need for my protective help would be.

"And the overland team: Christian Porter, Trey Larsen, and Zack Allman." I closed my eyes, barely registering the rest of his words. "The rest will remain with the main group. Main group men: please meet back here in thirty minutes to go over defense tactics. Small teams: please remain here for instructions. Dismissed."

So. Trek #2 for me would be just three guys, all of us young, and if they were anything like me, without much idea of what to do or how to survive. I firmed my lips. *Okay. I can do this. I can be a decoy and draw off the bad guys so the main group can get through. Yes.*

The captain said a few things to the three of us about how we'd need to pack carefully since we'd be traveling with only what we could carry in our saddlebags. There'd be places to resupply. We'd be taking a rural route, but we'd never be super far from people if we needed medical help or more food. I tried to let the news settle. *Okay. Okay.*

He said we'd need to exchange our uniforms for regular clothes, at least for now. I wondered why. If we were supposed to be a decoy, it seemed we should stay in uniform. But Captain Christensen said we were being watched pretty closely already. Changing into regular clothes wouldn't fool those people, but it would help us be more inconspicuous to any others we'd meet along the way.

I pulled jeans and a plaid flannel shirt from my saddlebags and put them on, feeling a bit sad to fold the uniform and tuck it away. Wearing it had made me feel more like I belonged, though I still felt like an outsider. *They're just clothes*, I told myself as I rebuckled the bags. *I'm still a soldier in the Legion. I'm just doing a little different job.* I looked around at the guys milling all over the camp. Still my comrades-in-arms. Still my brothers.

I knew Christian pretty well, having bummed around with him at the MTC. Definitely a cowboy, complete with the hat, Wranglers, and heeled boots. I'd seen Trey, but we hadn't gotten into a conversation or anything. He was lean and tanned, with dark hair and eyes. They both looked pretty excited, and I grinned back at them for solidarity. Everyone drifted off, but I sat tight, elbows on my knees, soaking it all in.

I felt a hand on my shoulder and looked up. The captain stood beside me, looking down with kind eyes.

"You all right, son?"

"Sure."

"Good." He looked around, his gray eyes flicking across the campsite, apparently assessing everyone's positions. "Because I'm making you the leader for the overland team. I've had my eye on you, and I know you're the man. And Zack, there's something else you should know. Keep this to yourself. There's no need to tell even the others on your team. But I think you ought to know: your team's cargo is *it*."

＋

The next morning my brain still felt scrambled from the news. Me, the team leader? I couldn't get my head around that. I'd tried to pray about it, to feel calm and sure of myself. I felt a little better but no instant answer there.

Captain Christensen pulled me aside as we finished packing up camp. "Gather your team. I want you ready to head out within the hour."

I gulped a little. Before I knew it, I'd be on my own. The one calling the shots.

"Get your men and help them choose supplies for yourselves. Make sure they get their saddlebags nice and balanced. You know what to do."

Did I? I'd certainly never done anything exactly like this before.

"When you're ready, come find me for final instructions."

I rounded up Christian and Trey, who were still pretty psyched about riding off together.

"So, guys, I guess I'm the leader for our team." I felt embarrassed saying so, but the captain had left that little announcement up to me. Maybe it was to be my first test of leadership. I tried to look confident and at ease, stuffing my hands in my pockets. But my worries were for nothing because the guys just grinned and set off a round of back-slapping. Actually, I think they were relieved someone else would be the decision-maker.

First test: pass.

At the supply wagon, we picked out some food and few other odds and ends like a first-aid kit, matches, horse grooming things, stuff like that. We piled it all on a picnic table, divided it into three stacks, and packed everything into our saddlebags, which already held our clothes and bedding. They bulged, to say the least.

"Okay, great. Now let's double-check our firearms." Each of us went over to our pile of tack, pulled our guns from their horse scabbards, and gave them a going-over. Christian seemed to know his way around a rifle, but Trey needed a little help.

"I've shot a rifle plenty, at targets and skeet," he said, his cheeks flushing. "But I gotta confess, my dad pretty much set it into my hands ready to go."

"It's no big deal," I said. "No worries. It's not that complicated. All right then. I gotta see the captain, and then we saddle up."

I walked over to where Captain Christensen stood looking over the horses.

"All set?"

"Yes, sir."

"Here's this." He held out a little stack of silver dollars. "You might be able to use them. You might not. It's not clear what state the towns along your way will be in. There are supply spots set up for you— the trip organizers did that via ham radio—but this is just in case." He tucked a packet of folded papers into my hand. "These are maps showing the best overland route with the supply spots marked. You'll see this means less miles for you than us, since you can go straighter, but rougher terrain since you won't be using the freeway like we are. Who knows? Maybe we'll arrive at the same time."

I grinned. "With all due respect, sir, I plan to beat you there."

He grinned back. "See that you do. For the most part, I'd guess the map-makers have picked the best path, but you've got leeway to alter your course if you think you should. The goal is for you to go as quickly and as inconspicuously as possible. That's why there are only three of you. Enough to back each other up but without the slowness that comes with a big group."

"Should I expect to be followed? Will we need to try to shake someone off our tail?"

"You should expect everything."

"As in, people shooting at us? You think that will happen?"

"It very well could." He crinkled his eyes into a squint, and I felt him size me up. His eyes fell to the handgun I wore in a side holster. "I noticed you have your own piece. That's a bit unusual. You've had some experience with it?"

"A bit."

"Are you prepared to shoot a man if necessary?"

That question. The one I'd been asking myself for months.

I looked back at him. "Yes, sir."

"Do you think you could kill someone if it came right down to it?"

"I already have."

I saw only the tiniest flare in Captain Christensen's eyes as he regarded me silently. He turned to the horses and caught Socks's bridle. "Let's get you on your way."

Captain Christensen dashed a look over each shoulder. From his jacket pocket he drew a small leather pouch and pressed it into my hand. "Carry this as you've seen me carry it."

I stuffed it into the inside breast pocket of my jacket, feeling a bulge roughly the size of a golf ball. "That's it? So small?"

"Yes. Small but worth everything. Many lives depend on it. It contains items that will allow the Church to recreate the cargo the cavalry unit is carrying, just in case. Your team has the best chance of getting through and getting there fast.

"Never let it out of your possession. Never let anyone even see it. When you get to Missouri, go to the Church's main compound. Ask for a man named Ben Young. That's who you need to deliver the pouch to. No one else."

I branded the name Ben Young on my brain. Mustn't forget.

I followed him back to the others, my heart pounding in my chest—just beneath where the pouch lay. I forced my hand to remain at my side, to not reach up and feel it nestled there.

We got situated and pulled ourselves into our saddles. Captain Christensen brought out a small satchel about the size of a Bible and tied it to the back of my saddle. He spoke quietly to us about it being the decoy and the necessity of treating it as if it were the most precious thing on earth. Christian and Trey nodded solemnly.

Captain Christensen gave me a piercing look. "You have our prayers," he said. "Don't forget to add your own."

CHAPTER FIVE

Amélie

HANDCARTS.

Could it really have come down to this?

Dad said there were vehicles, but with so many people, there just weren't enough to haul all our stuff. Handcarts would make up the difference. He explained there would be one animal-drawn wagon for each hundred people, which would carry tents and much of the food.

In typical Mormon fashion, preparing to roll out was super organized. The morning after the announcement, Dad and the boys reported to the stake center, where a mass handcart-building station was set up. Mom and I looked over our belongings. The weeding out process of what to take and what to leave would be way simpler this time, since we didn't own much.

We did have sheets and blankets besides the sleeping bags we'd used on the first trek. "We're taking every scrap of bedding we own," Mom said, "even if I have to carry it draped over my head. I have no idea how we'll stay warm enough at night."

I shivered just thinking about it, and right as I realized we didn't even own a tent, a lady from the stake knocked on our door, asking Mom and me to come to one of the ward buildings to help make tents.

Make tents? Okay.

Off we went. At the church, I walked into the gym. Numerous lamps of many kinds lit the room, and someone had even rigged one to hang overhead. I gaped at huge stretches of canvas spread across the gym floor. Women, girls, and a few men sat spaced out along their lengths, sewing seams.

A woman welcomed us, putting thick needles, thimbles, and spools of heavy thread in our hands. "This—these—are tents?" I stammered. "So big?"

"Sure are," she smiled. "People can use their own tents if they have them, but others will use these—a large circle with a pole in the middle, stakes around the edges. We jokingly call them "circus tents." Each tent sleeps twenty people." She motioned to one of the strips of canvas with people sewing all along it. "Pick a spot anywhere on this row." Some people sat on chairs, with the material draping up over their laps, and some sat right on the floor.

Mom reached out her hand to me. "Want me to thread your needle, honey?"

I knew how to sew—a little. Mom had taught me some basic mending, like sewing on buttons and such. Obviously, I knew how to thread a needle. I tried to quash the resentment that bubbled up inside. *She's only doing her motherly thing*, I told myself sternly. Even though I'm nineteen. She'll probably never stop doing it since I'll never stop being her "special" child, her hurt child.

"I got it," I said lightly.

She smiled with a shrug. My internal berating continued. *See?* I told myself. *Don't make everything a big deal. It's nothing.* It was only a moment, and that moment is over.

With a quick observation of the other people, I could see our task was quite simple. Thread the needle, tie a knot in the end. Sew in a straight line through two thicknesses. Mom fell happily to work, her hand flashing in, out, in, out. Once again, I had to grudgingly appreciate that years ago she'd embraced doing things by hand, and what once was an embarrassing eccentricity to me was now so useful.

We sewed for about three hours, and I had to admit I felt stiff all over and my fingers were super sore, despite the thimble, from pushing the needle through the heavy fabric. There's nothing wussy about "women's work," I decided. Mom and I hobbled home, knowing we'd have to return the next day. And possibly the next. Not fun, but the thought of traveling in wintery conditions would spur us on. We'd need those tents badly.

Dad, Ethan, and Jarron came home soon after, and we compared notes.

"The leadership told us that if more than two hundred thousand want to go, they may have to restrict the size of the first group," Dad said. "If they do, the criteria will be whether or not the family has their one-year food storage."

"But what about us?" Mom said in her panicky voice. "We haven't got any." She folded her arms tight across her chest and bit her bottom lip.

"But we did," Dad said, rubbing his palms along Mom's arms. "You know we did. We already gave it all to the Church when you left Zillah."

She nodded, but I could tell she struggled to keep smiling. After all, food storage had always been a point of pride—a place she could shine among her Mormon sisters, even if other things weren't quite right. But now she had no food storage at all.

"Don't forget, Mom. We loaded stuff out of the basement for hours. It was like a grocery store down there," Jarron said. "It's going to be okay."

I felt glad that Jarron joined in to buoy Mom up but a little sad at the same time that he'd realized that she needed it. He became less of a boy, more of a man in my eyes at that moment, and it seemed both a good and a sad thing.

"Oh yeah, they gave us those." Ethan pointed to two empty five-gallon buckets sitting on the floor in the corner. "We're supposed to have them on our handcart for water."

I thought about the big water truck we'd used on the first trek. They'd need a hundred of those this time with so many people, and I knew there was no way that was possible. "How's that going to work?" I asked.

"We're going to travel pretty close to rivers the entire time," Dad said. "We'll have to boil the water each night though."

—|—

The next day was more of the same. Building handcarts and sewing tents. Others helped with a myriad of tasks—I couldn't imagine the labor and coordination that would go into readying the food supplies. Any semblance of "regular" work was abandoned. I truly wondered what the people who weren't going with us were thinking. Didn't they worry there would be no civilized life after the Church pulled out?

What did the Ogden government think? There was no way they weren't aware—the whole city seemed upside down. It was completely obvious the Mormons were leaving—at least the core of them. Would they try to stop us? If they did, what would happen?

As I sewed, I thought about sleeping in a tent with twenty people. That didn't sound like much fun at all. I told myself that at least it would be better than hunkering down out in the open. I'd done that plenty of times on the first trek, but it had been summer—a completely different story.

That night, Dad and the boys brought home our handcart.

I stared at it. So small, even for a family who had next to nothing. We grouped around it, all of us speechless, looking into the cargo box. It was about three feet by four feet, roughly the size of a kitchen table. The wheels came up to my nose—about five feet. I slid my hand down the bar running across the front—here, my family would take turns walking, pushing, and pulling. Dad, Mom, Jarron, Ethan—but not me. I'd never be able to manage it with my leg. It'd be a miracle for me to merely make it on foot the whole way—forget pushing, pulling, or carrying. Once again, I was reminded that when it came to helping the family with physical tasks, I was pretty worthless. It had been that way on our farm, and it was that way now. As usual, I didn't say anything—just swallowed it all down.

Solemnly, Ethan set the two five-gallon buckets into the front of the cart. The remaining space was ridiculously small.

"It's not so bad," Dad said. "Mostly, we just need to carry our bedding and personal stuff, like clothes and cooking equipment. The food and tents will be on the company's wagon. So we don't need a lot of space."

"There's only one thing that's good about this trek, and that's the fact that you'll be with us this time," I said.

The next day, instead of sewing tents, Mom and I were asked to sew sacks of burlap—about the size that twenty-five pounds of potatoes came in at the grocery store, back when there was such a thing. Who knew what they'd be used for? Maybe potatoes. Meanwhile, Dad and the boys loaded trucks down at Welfare Square.

One more day. One more day to finish preparing, and then we'd leave Utah behind. We'd leave the West, where I'd lived my whole life. I doubted I'd ever see it again.

-+-

When we got home, I saw Cherilynn outside our apartment building.

"Hey!" I said. "I haven't seen you around lately."

"Yeah." She laughed. "Pretty crazy."

We sat down on the steps. "I've been dying to talk to you. I don't even know if you guys are going." There was no need to say where.

"Absolutely," she said. "My parents weren't positive at first, but we're all in now."

"Hard decision for them?"

"Sort of. They had to make sure it would be okay for me—that I'd be able to handle it."

I stared. "You?" I stammered before I could stop myself.

"Ha. I know what you're thinking. The varsity sports girl and everything. But actually, they're worried because I have a heart condition."

"You're kidding! You look healthy to me."

"It's no big deal, but my parents are super protective. As long as I take my medicine, I'm totally fine. I can do sports, whatever."

I couldn't help gaping at her. A heart condition? I guess you never know what problems people have hidden away. I looked at her and saw long, athletic legs, the flush of health on her skin. She seemed like she had everything I always wanted for myself physically.

"So your medicine controls it?"

"Yep. And once Mom and Dad confirmed the Church's drug supplies include plenty of my prescription, we were good to go."

I thought for a brief moment what it would be like if all it took was a little pill to take away my health problems, and then I felt ashamed. A limp isn't exactly a health problem, is it?

"Sweet. I'm really glad you're going," I said. "We can hang out, if you call walking all day hanging out."

She smiled. "Yeah. You can keep me going, since you're experienced at this trek stuff."

I started to laugh at the idea of me helping someone like her, and then I stopped myself. Maybe I could.

—+—

It happened. We left. We took our handcarts and oxcarts and trucks and tankers and walked out of Salt Lake City.

I heard there was a token attempt to stop us by the Ogden government, but I was isolated from that in my spot in the middle of the huge sea of people. Or, more likely, they weren't stupid enough to try to obstruct us. We were a boulder rolling down a mountain.

Or that's what I told myself. Logically, the food and supplies we carried were much too valuable to let go. The day of conflict was coming, and I couldn't imagine it going down easy. Many of the Mormons were armed. Dad had tucked two guns in our handcart—a rifle and a handgun. Who knew where he'd acquired them.

The road stretched in front of me, a perforated, undulating black ribbon. *I know all about this*, I thought, as I watched my feet *tap, tap, tap* down the freeway. *This I know.*

Maybe some things were different—like a hundred times more people. I'd thought we were a noisy bunch before, but the crazy cacophony of this group—a literal moving city—was beyond comparison.

Still, much was the same. Me, walking. Stepping out with my good leg, swinging my cane forward, hauling my bad leg after. Over and over. For hours.

My brothers flanked me, taking a break from their turn at our handcart, which Mom and Dad currently pushed. Beside us, someone's cow pulled a small cart. A little kid, maybe ten years old, held its halter, urging it along. Of course. What could be more normal these days?

"What do you call a cow with three legs?" Jarron asked, poking me in the ribs. He'd been telling me jokes all day, trying to get me to smile. Mostly, it worked. I couldn't resist his grin.

"Ok, what?"

"Lean beef." He laughed, leaning over and holding his skinny gut, the way only thirteen-year-old boys can laugh. Ethan, at fifteen, trying to act too cool for jokes, laughed anyway.

"Dad, where's the Nauvoo Legion in all this?" I asked.

"Toward the front, forming the vanguard. Soon they'll spread out along our flanks."

The front. I had no idea how far we were from the beginning of this endless train, but I knew it was farther than I could see. "So all I'd have to do is run super fast thataway, and I'd be able to see Zack?" I laughed so they'd know I was joking. Ha ha. Me, running.

Dad smiled. "Actually, even then you wouldn't see him."

"Why?"

"Found out this morning Zack has been assigned to a special company—a cavalry unit. They aren't traveling with the main group."

My heart sank into my stomach. Zack wasn't with us.

A cavalry unit? Was that dangerous?

"And you didn't think I'd be interested in hearing that?" I wanted to get mad at Dad, but it was pretty impossible when he was trudging along pushing the handcart, all stoic and uncomplaining.

"I only found out this morning as we were leaving, and they only told me because of us being like his kin. They don't spread that kind of news around. I was planning to tell you, but it goes without saying you should keep that to yourself. For his safety."

"Like who am I going to tell?"

I bit my lip to keep from crying. No way was I going to cry, not on the first day. But the disappointment stung. I'd really planned on laying my eyes on that boy. Soon.

I knew it was going to be crazy hard. But I told myself I'd already walked over seven hundred miles, and there was no reason I couldn't do it again. Whether or not I could make it another 1,100 miles was a question I didn't want to face.

I distracted myself by thinking about Zack. Maybe not a good idea since it made me miss him so much, but I succumbed to temptation.

The way I felt about him seemed as real as love could possibly feel. I knew how it wrenched my insides being apart from him. Still, the logical half of my brain asked, did I really know for sure? After all, I'd never been in love before. I'd never even had a boyfriend before. There was nothing to compare my feelings to.

The other half of my brain, the emotional one, said I didn't care if there hadn't been other boys. There's no way I could love someone more. Impossible.

A little niggling worry flitted in the corners of my mind. How can little Amélie possibly know for sure if she should take it to the next step and actually marry the guy? I mean, for me, that meant forever. Not just until things got hard or even just until death. How could I make a choice, in my youth and inexperience, that would last a million years and more? Way scary. Even the fact that I knew him better than nearly anyone on the earth didn't make that decision feel easy.

And besides, that choice wasn't upon me at this exact moment since Zack wasn't anywhere near—drat him. We hadn't talked about it much, other than a lot of clinging and promises to love. I felt a little ridiculous for even thinking about it. I sighed. Zack was off having adventures with the chances of him thinking of me down around 3 percent.

Amélie, this has to stop, I told myself. *Zack doesn't want an insane girlfriend.*

The rubber soles of my shoes slapped the pavement in an offbeat rhythm. The road inclined, working its way into Parley's Canyon. On the first trek, I continually worried about dropping back in the pack, about being last, about being made to ride the green truck with the old, sick people. Now the group was so impossibly large that, even after walking for hours, I couldn't see the front or the back. I had no idea what the plan was for people who couldn't walk. Surely there was a vehicle somewhere serving the purpose the green truck had—maybe the Bluebird and many more like it. Still, I had the feeling that if I couldn't keep up, my family would put me on the handcart.

That must not happen.

We walked until about five in the afternoon, when we arrived at Mountain Dell golf course—our first camping spot. The people around me looked plenty ready to stop. I knew many of them worried about how they'd be able to do this day after day. I'd felt the same way after my first day on the first trek. I felt that way now.

Men set up tall poles along the golf course's main road, signs attached to their tops. As I got closer, I saw the signs had the names of the various stakes on them: Sandy Utah East Stake. Murray Utah Parkway Stake. Centerville South Stake. A hundred of them. Several wagons stuffed with boxes and bundles pulled up beneath each sign.

"Ah, good," Dad said. "I'm in charge of a tent group, so I need to find our stake's wagons and help get stuff handed out."

"What's a tent group?"

"It's a group of twenty or so people assigned to one of the big tents. Each group has a leader who gets the tent and supplies from its designated wagon each evening. Each wagon holds five sets, enough for roughly one hundred people, and there are about fifteen wagons per stake."

My mind started to swim, thinking about how many wagons that would be overall. "How on earth did they find enough oxen and horses?"

"They were able to round up more than you'd think from the rural areas. Also, some of the stakes have been assigned trucks in place of a wagon or two."

The stakes' positions were roughly alphabetical, so after hiking a bit we found the Salt Lake Liberty Stake. Several wagons—and one very familiar blue truck—sat beneath it.

Tents of all sizes soon peppered the golf course. We sat down by the Bluebird to wait with Dad, who needed to stay at the pole until everyone in our tent group arrived.

"Dad, how did there get to be a million Mormons?" Ethan said.

He laughed. "A million? You're looking at maybe a hundred thousand. Only a tithing of a million."

"Didn't they say there would be two hundred thousand?" I asked.

"Yes. But a good percentage of them will be coming from Utah Valley, so they'll come up through Provo Canyon instead. Others will go through Ogden Canyon. We'll meet up later, where I-80 meets I-84, on the way to Evanston."

The idea that this ocean of people was only *half* the group wouldn't register in my mind.

Three families from our tent group arrived, joining us on the ground around our wagon. When the final family walked up, a zing of hopeful excitement spread through me. I recognized the teenage daughter.

"Cherilynn! You're in our tent group?"

She beamed back at me, but she looked as exhausted as I felt. "I guess so." She threw herself on the ground beside me. "Can I go ahead and die now?"

The dads and boys (there were five dads and seven boys, aged nine to sixteen) retrieved the bundle that would become our tent from the wagon, and the wagon master—our captain of one hundred—doled out a bag of dinner ingredients. I saw immediately what the burlap sacks we'd sewn were for.

"Be aware we'll need you back here in a few minutes to help dig the latrine trench," the wagon master said to the tent carriers.

The guys groaned. The females—Mom, the other four moms, Cherilynn, me, and a Primary-age girl named Janny—looked at each other with wide eyes. Perks of being a girl!

We found a spot to pitch our tent on the sixth hole near a sand trap, the once pristine green overgrown and yellowed. Cherilynn and I opened the bag of food to puzzle out how to transform it into a meal for twenty. We found a canning jar full of meat chunks and a couple handfuls of potatoes, onions, and carrots. Okay, stew then.

While we tried to figure out how to cut up vegetables with no countertop, we chatted.

"So do you have your eye on any of the guys in our stake?" Cherilynn nudged my elbow.

I laughed. "Err, no. I sort of have a boyfriend."

"You . . . sort of . . . ? How does that work?"

"Well, how do I explain this? We were—are—close, like really close. But he's in the Nauvoo Legion. So maybe it's weird to say he's my boyfriend when we're never together anymore. It's almost like he's a missionary."

She smiled. "You're not engaged, then? Or promised?"

I thought back to when he'd left for his training, when we said good-bye. The memory of his arms around me made me feel warm and safe. So strong. Yet gentle . . .

But Zack hadn't made it an official proposal or anything. It was all pretty vague. "Not exactly."

"What's he like, this semiboyfriend of yours?"

How to describe him? "Well, he's tall but not super tall. More average, really. Not all bulked up, more regular. Although, he's got these shoulders . . ." I grinned. "Blond but sort of brownish blond. And he's really nice, not stuck on himself. A little temper but not so as you'd notice." I wrinkled my nose. Everything I said, everything I could think of to say, was middle-of-the-road. There was no good way to encapsulate what Zack was like. He was ever so much more than middling.

"You love him. I can tell. You've got that look on your face. Big time." Cherilynn grinned.

"I admit it."

"Wasn't he worried one of the guys in this group would snatch you up during the long trip?"

"As if." I laughed. "Besides, who has time for romance when it's all we can do to make it to the end of the day?"

"Um, me." She grinned. "I can't wait to meet someone who will put that look on *my* face."

I dumped the contents of the canning jar into a big pot and broke the meat into pieces with a spoon. "How are you doing with your condition—your heart thing? Has it been a problem at all so far?"

"No problems. If I forget to take meds, my heart reminds me. It starts feeling fluttery and flip-floppy and weird, and I get light-headed. If I'm late taking it, sometimes it takes me a couple of hours to feel better, but it's part of my morning routine. So I feel pretty normal."

"Good, good."

While we finished preparing the food, the men and boys kept plenty busy: pitching our big, weird tent, cutting firewood (poor golf course trees), and digging that special trench. Portable johns with their reservoirs removed were then positioned over the trench. Lovely. Still, much better than nothing.

As evening began to fall, the glimmer of a hundred little campfires twinkled everywhere around us. Cherilynn and I sat on some big pieces of wood beside the fire, talking about this and that. I noticed Janny, the younger girl in our group, shyly watching us, twisting her long blonde braids in her fingers.

"Hey, Janny. Come sit with us," I said.

Her face brightened. "Really?"

"Of course. We've got a plush seat right here." Cherilynn patted the bumpy log beside us.

Janny scurried over and sat, beaming at us. I smiled, remembering how it had felt when older girls paid attention to me when I was a kid.

"How old are you, Janny?" I asked.

"Nine."

"Ah. You look pretty grown-up for a nine-year-old. Are you ready for this big adventure?"

"Sure," she said.

"Janny!" her mom called from the tent. "Time for your shot, honey."

"Shot?" I asked. "Ew! You have to have a shot?"

"Yeah," she said, smiling as she stood. "Insulin."

"Poor you," Cherilynn said. "Ouch."

"I'm used to it," Janny said. "I have to have one five times a day." She waved at us as she stepped away from the campfire. "See ya tomorrow."

"Gosh," I said. "Five shots a day. Not cool."

"It's cool that a shot handles it. Just imagine if we were real pioneers instead of fake ones. She'd never get to grow up," Cherilynn said.

We talked till the sun went down, the air becoming noticeably colder. *Here we go*, I thought. *We're going to be outside, solid, for the next three or four months.* The thought made me feel panicky. September nights in Utah would likely be nothing compared to Wyoming in October, and on from there. Our little campfire subsided into glowing coals, and soon it was dark. Really dark.

Mom pulled all the extra blankets out of our handcart, and we piled them on top of our sleeping bags. Then all twenty of us knelt on top of our bags and prayed together for safety, for a good night's rest. I let the warmth from everyone's good, faithful hearts sink into my bones. I didn't know most of these people yet, but I knew that before long, they'd become the most familiar faces in my life.

I climbed into my bag. Despite the weirdness of sleeping with twenty people—plus hundreds more very nearby—and the cold, lumpy ground, I felt myself drift off. One advantage to getting completely worn out—sleep came easily.

Day one. Done.

CHAPTER SIX

Zack

THE THREE OF US TOOK off cross-country. After most of the first day wore away, the quiet and isolation of the area really sank in.

We'd gotten pretty used to hearing only the creak of leather saddles and soft horse noises, so the sound of an engine approaching really stood out.

Could this be danger? Already?

"Come on," I said and nosed Socks farther back into the trees, hoping we wouldn't be seen. Christian and Trey followed.

A guy, probably in his late twenties, roared up on a four-wheeler, stopping not far from where we'd been. He looked around, confusion on his face.

He cut the engine, silence falling. "Hey, horse guys," he hollered. "Where'd you go? I just want to talk to you." He stood up, feet on the running boards, and held his hands high, facing away from our hiding place.

I peered at him. What could he want? How could an ATV be running after the EMP?

From my seat on Socks's back, I could plainly see he wasn't carrying any sort of cargo. If he had a weapon, it could only be somewhere on his person.

"Get out your rifles," I whispered. "I'm gonna talk to him, see what he wants. Cover me."

"Should you?" Christian whispered back. "We're supposed to go unnoticed."

"He's already seen us," I replied. I nudged Socks forward. He stepped delicately out of the trees, making very little sound. The guy didn't even hear us approach.

"What do you want?" I let my hand lay nice and easy on my handgun. The guy spun around, his lips making an O in the middle of his scruffy beard.

"Oh, hey," he said, smiling so his sunburned cheeks raised up nearly to his eyes. "There you are. Where's your friends?"

"Around."

"Yeah, well, hey. I don't mean to be a bother. I just thought maybe we could do a little business." His smile seemed a little too wide.

"What are we talking?"

"You boys seem to be in a bit of a hurry. So I've got a deal for you. You see this here four-wheeler?" He stepped off and flourished a hand. "It's in great shape. I know a guy who can resurrect engines like this without too much trouble, and I've got a couple more four-wheelers I can put my hands on just like it. How about we have ourselves a trade? Straight across, even though we all know four-wheelers are valuable right now, quite valuable—more than a horse, anyway."

"Trade?" I scrunched my eyebrows. "You want our horses?"

"You know you'd make better time with these." He patted the back end of the machine. "Never gets tired. Never needs feed."

"You've got a point there," I said. "But they do need gas. And that's the problem, isn't it? Gas is pretty much impossible to find."

"Oh, you can find it if you look. It may take a little effort, but I doubt you'd have serious problems. Think of how much faster you could move."

I thought about it for one fine moment. I thought about racing over the miles, getting the super-important, super-secret package to Missouri in days instead of months. That would be good, wouldn't it? And I'd be done with this mission so I could get back to what I really wanted to do, which was be with Lee. Make sure she was okay.

My eye drifted over the machine, which, although it had sounded okay a minute ago, could have any number of problems. What exactly had the guy done to get it running? If it broke down, where would we get parts? What if it got a flat?

A few facts settled on my mind. The Church had meticulously planned this mission and worked hard to give it the best possible chance of succeeding. I suppose they could have put us on four-wheelers, but they chose horses instead. I had to trust that they knew better than I about what we faced.

"Thanks for the offer, but I'm going to pass," I said.

"Now think this through. You've got a long way to go."

My insides prickled with warning. How did he know we had a long way to go? The whole thing started to feel even more suspicious. I peered at him. His eyes slid from mine to the trees, apparently searching for my companions.

"Sorry. I'll be on my way." I turned Socks toward the mountain path, angling away from where Christian and Trey hid.

The guy put a couple of fingers in his mouth and whistled, a loud, piercing shriek. Three other guys came over the hill—two on ATV's, one on horseback.

"See now, we've got an ATV for each of you. I know you've got two buddies. It'll work out just right." I noticed the new guys had guns lying across their laps. I firmed my lips. He'd never intended to trade. This was a "take."

Letting my loop of reins drop, my hand tightened around my gun. I raised it, pointing it at the first guy and supporting it underneath with my other hand. "Tell your friends to stay where they are."

"Back off!" Christian yelled from the trees. I cringed at the sound. He'd given away their position.

I heard the crack of rifle shot, coming from much higher up the mountainside. My heart thudded. They had men up there too? We'd be easily surrounded.

At first I couldn't see where the shot was aimed, but then the guys on the new ATV's started swearing. The shot had pierced one of the tires. One of them aimed his rifle up the mountain where the sound had come from, but as he did so, another shot rang out. Another tire hit.

What was going on? Who was up there?

The first guy swore. "Forget it. Let's get out of here."

"Should we follow him?" one of the ATVers said, pointing at me.

"Can't fit through there," the first guy said.

"I could," the one on horseback countered.

"Forget it. They've got us pinned down." He turned the machine around and roared off, apparently to find easier game.

I sat tense in the saddle. Who were the sharpshooters who'd shot out those tires? Why had they helped us? What did they intend to do now?

I saw Christian on his horse come out of the trees and move toward me.

"Where's Trey?" I asked.

"Up there." Christian waved a vague hand up the mountainside. "You heard the shots."

"Wait. That was Trey?" I said, dumbfounded. "Sounded like two shooters."

"Nope. Just Trey." Christian's horse nosed mine. "He was moving around up there pretty good."

Trey and his horse came out of the trees and rode up next to us. I gaped at him. "That was crazy amazing, man," I said. "Who knew you could shoot like that? I guess target shooting with your dad did some good."

Trey smiled and holstered his rifle. I noticed he seemed comfortable handling it, much more so than when I'd showed him how to clean it. Odd.

The horses picked their way up the stony trail. "I've got a very weird feeling about those guys," I said. "Seemed like they knew too much about us."

Trey looked at me and then reined around the way we'd come. "You guys keep going. I'll be right back."

I started to say, "Where are you going" or maybe "You shouldn't go off by yourself," but before I could, he galloped away.

I thought I'd go crazy because Trey didn't reappear for three hours. At last, we heard the clop of galloping hoofbeats on rock, and there was Trey coming up the trail behind. I noticed his saddlebags overflowed, and he even had a bag sitting across his lap.

"What was that all about?" I asked when he reached us.

"Just tying up a couple of loose ends." He smiled with one side of his mouth.

"Is that all you've got to say about it?"

"Let's talk about it when we camp."

I looked at Christian, who shrugged. I decided to leave him be for now, but Trey was a question I wanted an answer to.

+

Our path was mountainy and slow going, but it was nice having water right at hand for the horses, in a creek that flowed in the rocky banks. Whenever a meadow opened up, we took the chance to canter or gallop the horses. We kept that up for the rest of the day, and then we found a sheltered spot under the trees to camp.

According to the map, we'd managed about twenty miles. Not bad—especially considering the scare with the ATV guys—but not great either.

We made a small fire and rolled a couple of fallen logs over to sit on. After we got the horses settled, Christian and Trey headed out to round up some extra firewood. I put a small pot over the coals and dumped in a couple of cans of stew, all the while watching my companions' heads as they bobbed out of sight. I sank to a seat on a log and pulled the little bundle from my jacket pocket.

That pouch had bounced up and down next to my chest all day, tantalizing me, but until now there hadn't been a single chance to look at it unseen. I hefted it on my palm. So small. I couldn't imagine what it contained that was so important.

I wiggled the drawstrings loose until I could peer inside. A plastic zipper bag held a dark mass that gave when I pressed on it. I zipped it open and delicately put my fingers inside. Another, slightly smaller zipper bag. Okay.

There was a small vial of liquid in its own little bag, and a tiny memory card like the ones we used to fit into a camera or cell phone, back when there were such things. And then there was a bag holding hundreds of small brown kernels.

Wheat. But somehow more.

I grinned. I was like Jack and the Beanstalk. I had a bag of magic seeds.

+

I tucked the pouch away, and the others returned.

"Okay, out with it," I said to Trey. "What did you go back to do? And I can tell when a guy knows how to handle a gun, and you do. Why did you pretend you didn't?"

Christian's face lit with curiosity, but he said nothing.

"I went back just to double-check we weren't being followed. We aren't. Right now, anyway." His face went grim, and I wondered just exactly what he did to "double-check."

"As for the gun thing, I was told not to talk about my experience, not until we were well under way, and even then to use discretion. I was told that if we never had trouble and it didn't come up, there'd be no reason to mention it."

"Wait. Who told you?" I asked. This didn't make any sense. I thought I was the only one in the group who had a secret.

"One of the leaders setting up this mission. He thought it best to keep knowledge of my background quiet so it wouldn't draw attention to our team. They want us to look as insignificant as possible, you know. Just three guys."

"Your background?"

"Yeah, well, here we go. Before the attacks, I was active military. An Army Ranger."

"Whoa!" Christian said. "How old are you, man?"

"Twenty. One of the youngest to graduate the program. Actually, I'd just completed my first tour when the world came apart."

"So the leaders thought if anyone knew a Ranger was assigned to the team that there must be something special about it. So they kept it quiet," I said.

"Pretty much," Trey replied.

"But we're the decoy," Christian said. "Maybe it would make us a better decoy if that was known. They'd take us more seriously." We all glanced at the satchel tied on the back of my saddle—the pretend cargo.

"They want us to be a distraction but not attract too much attention since we're just three guys," Trey said. "They want us to stay alive."

I clenched my teeth. Should I say anything about the pouch in my pocket? Would that make it safer or in more danger? I remembered Captain Christensen's words—"Don't show it to anyone." Maybe Trey knew about it already anyway. He'd obviously talked to someone pretty high up, after all. I opened and shut my mouth a few times.

"Plus, maybe our mission is more important than just a decoy," I blurted.

"What do you mean? What's in the satchel?" Christian said.

I shook my head. "A Bible. That's it. I'm just saying we don't know the whole picture."

"Yup," Trey agreed.

"So, Trey, seeing as how you have all this training, it seems only logical that you be the team leader. Only makes sense. I'm completely okay with that," I said. "Actually, I'd prefer it."

Trey raised his hands. "Oh no. No. Sorry. That's not my skill set. Besides, the Church contact was very specific about that. You're supposed to remain the team lead."

My stomach twisted. "I don't get it. Why? Why me? I'm younger than you. I don't have your experience. I got nothing." The moment the words left my lips I regretted it. I knew I needed to remain strong. But it was the bald truth. Sure, I knew how to ride, I could shoot (although nothing like Trey), and I had my previous experience with Trek #1. But I was raw as they come in so many ways—especially about Church things.

I believed. Maybe that was enough. At the moment, though, all I felt was young and scared.

"The guy didn't have time to go into a lot of detail," Trey said.

"Well, it still seems like you're the obvious choice."

Trey just smiled—that smile he often wore, the one that was starting to get on my nerves since it seemed to mean, "I have nothing more to say."

"Okay, look," I said. "I know someone has to be the final say on stuff, but I hope you guys will be straight with me and tell me when I'm being ridiculous. You gotta help me. I'd rather we work decisions out between us."

"Sure, bro," Christian said.

"Yup," Trey said. "But in the end, you're the guy. We gotta be clear on that."

I took a deep breath. "Okay. So tell us what happened when you took off."

"I was pretty sure those ATV guys weren't working on their own, and I didn't think it would be a good idea for them to report back on our whereabouts. I found their camp, where they were trying to repair their tires. The guy on horseback didn't seem to be around, though, which worries me. Let's just say the guys on the ATVs have a very long walk back to civilization. Long enough that we'll be long gone."

"Er . . . what exactly did you do to them?" Christian asked.

"One of them got knocked out pretty good. The other two I just tied up. Took all their shoes, too, just to slow them down a bit. I pitched those down a ravine along the way. I confiscated their weapons and their radios. All military issue."

"They're military?" I asked in disbelief.

"Yup. If you can call it that. They're part of the Ogden faction. Tattoos and all."

"Their radios work? I'd have thought they'd have fried."

"Those guys are squatting at Hill Air Force Base, so they have access to the military's stuff. The air force had special shielded containers where they kept spares of certain things—in case of an EMP. So, yes, they have a few radios and other replacement items."

"So what now?"

"Continue as planned, but be on guard. If you agree. I'm pretty sure there's a weasel in the cavalry company that told the Ogden people where to look for us. We'll run into them again, no doubt."

—+—

We continued on the steep, rocky trail overhung with gnarled scrub oak. Brush swept the horses' flanks and our legs. But after a couple of hours, the way opened up into a wide meadow. We didn't have to do much urging to get the horses to gallop after spending so much time clambering up an ankle-breaking path. The number of trees thinned, and gradually the landscape flattened, reminding me of our Trek #1 through southern Idaho. I didn't like how exposed we were, but there was nothing to do about it.

The Ogden government was after us. It seemed a bit halfhearted at this point, but the thought chilled me. Could we avoid being tracked? The map showed back roads and small state highways, but we'd have to stay off those, using them just for guidance. How would I know what to do?

As I rode, I prayed. *Our Father who art in heaven . . .* I still kept the old way of praying I'd acquired as a young Catholic—sort of a mumbling mutter, just under my breath. Amélie said it was okay—she said the important thing was to make sure prayer was part of my life, not so much how or where I did it. That made sense to me. She told me I'd get better at it over time. I was plenty glad to hear that. If a guy ever needed help, I did.

Over the next few days, we traveled through a lot of plain, empty country. We didn't see many people, and those we did see were at a distance. We shadowed the state highway in the area—nothing more than a little two lane road with only a couple of stalled cars sitting on it. We rode a few hundred yards to the side.

Finally, on the fifth day out from Jordanelle, the map directed us to stop at a little farmstead. This was to be our first resupply spot. I looked forward to seeing and talking to someone new—especially someone who was involved in helping us fulfill our mission.

The thought of some different food in our supply bags sounded good too. But would everything be on the up-and-up?

We rode into the yard. There was a squatty white house surrounded by a few spindly trees. A barn and shed stood in the back. A row of four rickety-looking horse trailers fronted a corral. In spite of how old and rusted the trailers looked, the horses trotting around the corral looked like fine beasts.

I sat looking at the house, not sure what to expect. Here we were. Now what? I looked over at Trey. He smiled that same smile.

I slid off Socks's back, looped the reins over a tree branch, walked up, and knocked on the door. I hoped I wouldn't need the handgun tucked in the back of my waistband.

I stared at the door's weathered paint, wondering what I'd say when the door opened. Hopefully I was at the right place and the person would know exactly what was to happen next. I wondered vaguely if we should have some secret password to give each other.

A willowy woman in her middle years with long, gray hair—like a smooth horse tail—opened the door.

"Yes?" she said, looking me up and down, taking in my dust-stained shirt and jacket, the hems of my jeans caked with mud. Her eyes passed from me to Christian and Trey, still on horseback.

"Uh . . . " I stammered.

"You're the church boys," she said and laughed, the gray ponytail flicking back and forth. "I'll fetch Hyrum. We've been expecting you." She stepped onto the porch, shutting the door behind her. "I'm Annie. Come on around back. He'll be in the shed."

"Ma'am." I nodded.

Hyrum. Okay. I'd never heard that name before joining the Church. Somehow it made me feel better as I went to meet this stranger. I knew I needed to still be wary, but it wasn't just the name that made me feel okay about trusting these people. There was more—a good feeling that this was right. We'd be okay putting ourselves in their hands.

I walked back to Trey and Christian. "How does this feel to you guys? Seem good? Seem right?"

Christian nodded. Trey said, "Stay on your toes, but, yes."

"Bring your horses with you," Annie called out. I led Socks after her, and Christian and Trey followed.

Hyrum turned out to be the male version of Annie, with long, slender limbs and gray hair, though his ponytail only brushed his collar.

"Hello, hello," he said, swiping his hands against his pant legs and then reaching for our outstretched hands. "Let's settle your horses with some proper feed, and then we'll talk."

"Oh, uh, I wasn't sure if we were to quickly resupply and be on our way or—" I broke off.

"Of course you're to stay. Tomorrow morning is plenty soon enough to be back on the road. Steaks sound okay?"

Trey, Christian, and I grinned at each other. That sounded more than okay.

Hyrum insisted on helping us unsaddle the horses and turn them into the corral. Then we filled the troughs with hay, grain, and water.

—+—

I'd never tasted steaks like that before. Celestial steaks for sure. Maybe it was because I'd been eating the plainest sort of trail food for the last several days, making any "real" food taste heavenly, or maybe it was because Hyrum raised the beef himself. Either way, we gorged ourselves until Hyrum and Annie both laughed at the spectacle.

After dinner I worried that our hosts might try to get information from us—that they might feel they deserved it after giving us their best hospitality. What would I say if they pressed me? I didn't know *much*, but I did have a couple of secrets to keep.

My worry was for nothing. They told us what they knew about the road ahead—sounded like a whole lot of nothing—and showed us to our beds. After only the hard ground for days, the mattress felt like a cloud. I fell instantly asleep.

In the morning, after a delicious breakfast of bacon and scrambled eggs, we repacked our saddlebags with cans of meat and beans, packets of dried soup, jerky, cocoa mixes, dried fruit, and any other good things we could fit in the nooks and crannies. Good thing I liked oatmeal!

We walked out to the corral to get the horses ready. Hyrum reached the gate first and turned. "Boys, no need to argue over which horse you'll take. They are all fine mounts, every one. Just choose one that suits you."

"What do you mean? We'll just go on with our horses we came in on," I said.

"Of course not. Didn't they explain this to you? You're to have fresh mounts at every supply stop. You've got a long way to go, and without trading for rested horses, it would take way too long."

Stunned, I simply gaped at him. "Well, no one mentioned that detail." At first, I wondered if it might be some kind of trick. But what Hyrum said made sense, and there was no real reason why exchanging one good horse for a more rested one wouldn't be a good idea.

Sadly, it had gotten hard to trust people.

"What do you guys think about this?" I asked Christian and Trey.

"I expected it," Trey said.

Christian shrugged then nodded.

Well, okay. Reluctantly, I stepped into the corral and walked up to Socks. "Good-bye, boy." I stroked his neck, and he nuzzled me back.

Would nothing in my life stay the same?

The moment I had the thought, I felt ashamed. I had the Church now, or rather, I had the Savior. He wasn't going anywhere. He was there for me forever. And I was there for Him. I knew I was only beginning to learn this, and maybe it would take a lifetime to understand. Still, I knew God wouldn't change. That was something to cling to.

My thoughts drifted to Lee. What about her? Would she break my heart and join the list of things that changed? I wanted her in my life more than I wanted anything. But wanting wasn't having. Did she think about me? All I could do was hope.

I looked at the horses in the corral. Yes, they looked good. Strong, spirited, all of them. But one, an all-black gelding, stood apart from the others. Definitely the best horse.

I walked over. He started to shy away from me, but when I looked him in the eye, he stood still. I caught his halter and led him to the gate.

Maybe it wasn't quite kind to nab the best horse. At the moment, though, I couldn't make myself pass him up. And besides, me and Big Black weren't going to be staying together long. I wouldn't be forming a relationship with him—just until the next supply stop. In a few days, I'd have to leave him behind, like so much else in my life.

Ten minutes later we galloped out of Hyrum and Annie's yard under cold, empty skies. I realized I'd never been this far away from my old home in Zillah before. That notion might have been more fun if I thought I'd ever see home again.

+

The next day was Sunday. We'd camped in a pretty little wood next to a stream, and the morning dawned bright, clear, and a bit cold. The scrub oak and aspen surrounding us wore a gorgeous mixture of green, yellow, red, and orange.

We arose and went through our regular morning motions—seeing to the horses, getting a cookfire going, heating water, cooking oatmeal. I wished I'd had clearer directions on what I was supposed to do for Sundays. Well, I hardly had any directions *period*. But nothing was said about what standard Sabbath procedure should be. On the first trek, we always stayed put. We had church meetings with the whole stake and more or less used it as a day of rest. But what was I supposed to do now? I felt we should rest—not just because I was exhausted but because it seemed like the right thing to do. But what would the others think? Maybe they'd think I was being ridiculous. Didn't we need to travel as quickly as possible?

I *so* didn't want to be the one to make the call. But I knew I had to. I was the team lead. We hadn't even discussed it, so the other two would probably be taken by surprise when I told them we weren't moving out. I felt a hundred kinds of awkward.

What would Lee do? I guessed she'd probably pray about how to handle it. I sighed. This was all so new and difficult—even after three months of being a Mormon.

I couldn't make myself kneel down, not when the other guys would see me. I knew I was being prideful, but I wasn't to the point where I could do that, at least not yet. I bowed my head.

Our Father who art in heaven, hallowed be thy name . . . My fingers itched to hold my rosary beads. Prayer had been such a simple matter before I joined the Church. Do this. Say that. Now say this.

I sent up a wordless plea for help. It wasn't hard mustering up humility since I felt completely small and helpless.

The thought came that even though we'd lose a day's travel, we'd be able to move more quickly come Monday after having rested. The horses needed rest too.

Hmm. Maybe that was the tack to take. It even sounded semilogical.

Was that an answer to prayer? I wasn't sure. It felt right though.

"Hey, uh, guys, what do you think of staying here today?" I stammered. "It being Sunday and all."

"Is it?" Christian said. "I totally lost track of days."

Trey grunted. "Stay here? A whole day? You know we gotta move fast."

I swallowed. "That's what we did on the other trek, and it seemed to work out. We can use the rest. And my horse is beat after carting my carcass around."

"Did Captain Christensen tell you we should stop on Sundays?" Trey asked.

"No. He didn't say anything about it."

"Huh." Trey turned back to rolling his bedding. "Your call."

I cringed inside. I could tell he didn't love the idea. "What do you think, Christian?"

"Fine by me."

Would I ever get used to being the one making the final decisions on things? I had no experience doing it. Dad had always been there before everything happened. The two of us, together. Him calling the shots. Me following his lead.

Silence stretched out. Trey and Christian looked expectantly at me.

"We'll stay," I finally decided. "Let's get some rest. We can nap a bit during the day and get started before dawn tomorrow. We can make up some time that way. Plus, we can travel for a while under cover of darkness just in case someone's watching for us."

Trey didn't say a word. He unrolled his just-rolled bedding and stretched himself out on it, pulling his hat down and folding his arms across his chest. In only a moment, I heard the sounds of the deep, even breathing of sleep.

I stood there looking at him, unsure about what to do next. Christian stepped up beside me. He joshed me with his elbow, and when I turned, he grinned at me. I grinned back.

"It'll be good," he said quietly. "Don't worry."

"Thanks."

"You gonna preach us a sermon?"

I sputtered a laugh. "As if. I wouldn't know the first thing about how to do that." Slowly another smile spread across my face. "I get to make assignments, right? You do it."

Christian snickered. "Okay, here you go: to be at one with God, it helps to be at one with nature." He spread his arms wide. "We're doing that pretty darn good."

"I've got *nature* all over my boots." I scraped some horse dung off with a stick.

We fell into a comfortable silence, soaking in the beautiful fall colors surrounding us. I couldn't help thinking about Lee. What was she doing right now? Was she okay?

"Hey, so, do you have a girl back home? Or in the big group?" I asked.

"Naw. I'm not the boyfriend type."

I laughed. "The boyfriend type? What is that, anyway?"

"You know, sticking with one girl. I like to be a free agent. Not that there are many girls to choose from in my little town. How 'bout you? Are you the boyfriend type?"

"I didn't think I was. But yeah, I've got a girl. At least, I hope I do."

"What do you mean, you hope?"

"Last time I saw her, we were tight. But now, well, we're a long way apart. I hope she remembers me."

"Where is she?"

"In the main encampment."

"What's she like? It goes without saying she's gorgeous, of course."

"Of course. Long, soft hair. Pretty eyes—" I broke off. It bugged me that I started to say she had a limp, as if it was a defining characteristic. "She's amazing. I've known her since we were kids. We grew up together."

"Aww, now you're killing me with cute." Christian laughed. "What's her name?"

"Amélie." How long since I said her name aloud? I tried to savor it—her name, our memories, the essence that was so uniquely her.

Christian looked squarely at me. "She'll remember you. No doubt about it."

+

Monday morning we set out before dawn.

"While you two were playing Sunday School, I went for a walk," Trey said as the horses settled into a rhythm. "Found a nice overlook and spent some time watching for signs of being followed. Turns out we are."

"Uh-oh," Christian said.

"But thanks to Sunday School and that creek we crossed a couple of times, they've lost our trail and actually gotten ahead of us." He smiled.

Maybe now Trey won't be super ticked about us resting a day, I thought. In the hours and hours we'd spent together, riding, camping, surviving, I'd felt a closeness starting to spring up between the three of us, and I really didn't want to mess that up. It'd been so long since I felt like I really belonged. As nice as having friends was, that was really just a great side benefit. We needed to be solid in order to fulfill our mission.

Just before noon, Christian cried out, "Aw, crap." He swung from the saddle.

"What's wrong?" I said. Both Trey and I dismounted.

"Here, hold these." He handed me his reins. Carefully, he felt his horse's left front leg and then lifted it, looking at the hoof. "Nutmeg's pulled up lame."

While I held Nutmeg, he rooted around in his saddlebags for a hoof pick. I watched in quiet admiration as he skillfully picked out the horse's hoof. A stone had lodged there, but Christian soon had it out, along with another smaller one.

"She's going to be tender for a while," Christian said, taking the reins back. "I'll lead her for now." He took off walking, keeping to softer ground, Nutmeg at his heels.

"Here," I said. "We can ride double and trade off walking if we need to."

"I'm good," Christian called over his shoulder. "Looks like you all will need to work at keeping up with me."

We hadn't even gone a mile before Trey pointed at the highway we were shadowing, a few hundred yards to the right. "Look at that."

A group of twenty, maybe thirty people walked down the road. The area we were crossing through didn't have much cover, so they saw us as well. They were mostly men, but a few women dotted the crowd. They started yelling and broke toward us, leaving the roadway at a dead run.

"What the heck?" I said.

"Get ready. Those are desperate folks, and they'll do pretty much anything to get supplies. I hope they aren't armed," Trey growled, cocking his rifle. "If they start shooting at us, I'll have to kill them, and I'd rather not."

Thirty people vs. Trey? I had no doubt he could take care of it.

I grabbed my rifle from its holster. With Nutmeg lame, we couldn't make a run for it.

Trey snapped his reins. "Yah!" He galloped toward the group, firing a warning shot over their heads. Most of the people staggered back in confusion, turning to run back the way they'd come. Two hesitated then started running toward us again. Wow. Desperate.

Maybe fifty yards off, Trey fired again, right at their feet, kicking up a puff of dust. At that, they also turned back.

Trey returned to our sides. Christian and I drew big breaths of relief. "Good grief," I said. "I feel terrible for them. They must be starving."

"They are," Trey said, watching them resume their walk down the highway. "But we can't help them. Our mission must come first. And even if we gave them all our food, it wouldn't go far among all those people. Wouldn't really help them and just mess us up."

"You're right, of course," I said. I wondered how many more groups there were like that, walking across the country—probably city people who left after the EMP, feeling they had gotten out in the nick of time, only to face a different kind of danger out here.

In late afternoon we found a bit of cover and made camp early to give Nutmeg a little extra rest. Christian thought she'd be good to go tomorrow, and we'd need to make up time. The urgency of our mission pressed down on me, and the slowness of our progress drove me nuts. I had no idea what I'd do without Christian and Trey to keep me moving forward.

CHAPTER SEVEN

Amélie

THE SIGHT OF THE VARIOUS groups converging at the crossroads to Evanston was astounding. When we got to a bit of higher ground and could look out over the landscape, the sheer numbers—the ocean of people without beginning or end—blew my mind. Yet the fact that the main company was twice as big now boggled my mind but didn't change the course of my days, filled with walking, walking, and more walking. It seemed like there should have been some fanfare though. Never before in modern times—and perhaps ever—had such a group traveled together.

Our handcart rolled smoothly down the freeway, and despite the fact that we continually climbed in altitude, I knew this was a piece of cake compared to pushing through deep sand or mud, like the pioneers. Having a nice hard surface was definitely easier. Dad, Ethan, and Jarron did most of the pushing, although Mom jumped in often. Being a farm family, they were used to physical labor. At the end of the day, they were plenty tired, but I could only imagine how difficult this had to be for the legions of pencil-pushers and moms in this group. I felt terrible that I couldn't help push, but I couldn't do anything about it.

Maybe the carts rolled smoothly but definitely not quietly. The sound of our passage was more like a roar. The squeak and creak of hundreds of carts added to the rumble of wheels, along with the hubbub of animals plodding along, people walking, talking, shouting, laughing, babies crying, and somewhere, though not near me, the sound of trucks—real trucks with real combustion engines. I was surprised at the number of horse- or oxen-drawn wagons there were, all overflowing with supplies. Some little kids rode bikes, and a few older people too.

I smiled when I saw some people going super gung-ho with pulling. Some guys were almost *running* with their cart. Yeah, it looked like a pride thing, and there was some of that going on, but once those guys arrived at the next campsite, they'd park their carts and come back to help the ones who were struggling.

It was sort of funny how people naturally kept their old highway habits. The slower carts stayed to the right, while the left side of the road became a fast lane of sorts. I heard them call "On your left," just like road racers.

Every now and then we'd come upon dead cars, just like we did on the first trek. Sometimes they'd pulled to the side, but often they sat right in the middle of the lane. I could picture how confused the drivers must have been when their cars just suddenly stopped working. They must have thought they ran out of gas or something, but then they'd see that everyone else's cars had also stopped. No doubt they tried and tried to get things going again, and they'd have finally just abandoned their vehicle and walked a very long way out of here. How weird and scary that must have been.

Our handcarts and wagons flowed around these infrequent islands of cars, trucks, semis, and so on as we came to them. Once in a great while, people found things of use in the semis, but usually they'd either been looted or the stuff wasn't any good anymore. One truck they opened was stuffed full of expensive flat-screen televisions. Worthless. Another was stacked with cases of what used to be lettuce. Gross.

One thing surprised me a little: as far as I could tell, "outsiders," or people who weren't part of our big group, didn't try to hassle us or anything. I guessed it was because our group was so ridiculously big. Plus armed. Trying something on us would be like yanking a lion's tail.

Cherilynn walked beside me. "It's too bad there wasn't time to work on that assignment you had from the Church. Sounded like it would have been fun."

"Actually, I'm still supposed to do it."

"Really?" She choke-laughed. "How?"

"Want to help me figure it out? Unless you're busy, ha ha."

She grinned. "I guess there's no reason we couldn't do it. Just like we planned before—find people to help, work our way through everyone."

"It actually might be even easier on the trek," I said. "After all, if you think about it, people are closer together now than in their houses. There are about one hundred stakes. Think we could try to visit one or two per night?"

"Yeah. No problem. We won't be tired or anything."

I showed her the fat notebook I'd brought along to use for this project. "How about we take the list of stakes, put the first one at the top of a page in this notebook, then skip a few pages and put another stake's name, and so on. Then when we visit a stake, we can put all the names in with their interests and stuff."

"Sounds good," Cherilynn said. "When we get helpers, they can just write it down on paper and then turn it in to you. Then we recopy it into this master book."

"And if we meet someone while we're walking in the daytime, we can always go ahead and talk to them. Sort of a little head start." I turned to scan the people walking behind us.

A guy, maybe fifteen or sixteen, rode by on a bicycle. "Hey, wait," I called. He turned, surprised, and braked to a stop.

"Hi, I'm Lee," I said as I limped up to him. Cherilynn trailed me. "I'm doing a survey. Want to help?"

"A survey?" He laughed. "Now?"

"I know. Weird, huh?" I grinned. "It's actually for the Church."

He looked at me with one eyebrow raised.

"No, really, it is," Cherilynn said.

"I have a letter from them to prove it, in my stuff," I waved at our handcart.

"It's okay." He climbed off his bike, and we began to walk together. "What's the survey?"

"Just a couple of questions about your talents and interests. What stake are you in?"

"Bountiful East Stake."

"Ok, hang on a sec." I hooked my cane over my arm and flipped a few pages into the notebook. If I was to write stakes on pages alphabetically, I'd need to go about ten pages in for the B's. Using Cherilynn's back as a writing surface, I wrote "Bountiful East Stake" across the top of the page.

We talked to him for a while, writing down his name and interests. The best part was he said he'd help us in the evenings and knew others who'd brought bicycles. They'd be able to act as messengers and traverse the area more quickly—at least, as long as their bikes lasted. After the initial supply of spare tubes was gone, if they broke down or got flats, it would be pretty hard to fix them.

"See ya tonight." He waved and sped off, weaving around the walkers.

New friends. People to talk to. Helping the Church. Win, win, win.

I looked over my shoulder to see a group of ten men dressed in the uniform of the Nauvoo Legion walking up along our flank. I felt a stab of loneliness at the sight. If Zack hadn't been put into that special, mysterious group, that might have been him. Why did it seem the world conspired to keep us apart?

"It's true what they say about guys in uniform," Cherilynn said. I pressed my lips together. I'd never even gotten to see Zack in his.

One of the riders looked very familiar as he drew closer. I'd know that mop of dark curls anywhere.

Ryan Cook. I hadn't seen him since we arrived in Salt Lake. I wondered what he'd been up to. Playing his guitar and singing, I guessed. But that didn't pay the bills. Not anymore. And now he was a soldier.

"Ryan!" I called and lifted a hand in greeting. His face lit up, and he stopped once he got to us. The others in his group flowed past.

"Hey, baby. How's it going?" He gave me a hug, squeezing me tight. *Almost* brotherly.

I managed not to blush. "Good. I'm good. So you're in the Legion, huh?"

"Yes, ma'am." He smiled that poster-boy smile and put his hands on his slim hips, almost as if he was proudly drawing attention to the sidearm holstered there. And yes, that uniform looked pretty amazing on him. I couldn't help smiling back.

Cherilynn nudged me. "Is that your boyfriend?" she whispered. "No, wait, you said he had lighter hair." I looked sidelong at her, grinning. Clearly, his smile had done its magic on her as it had so many others—including me, at one time.

"Cherilyn, meet Ryan Cook," I said.

"Hey," she said. It amused me greatly to watch Ryan's face as he realized she had no idea he was somebody famous.

He recovered quickly. "Hey, yourself. So, how do you know Amélie?"

"We're in the same stake. How about you?"

"Funny, that. We used to be in the same stake back in Washington." He slung his arm across my shoulders. "Amélie, can you believe we're doing this trek thing again?"

"I know, right?" I glanced ahead to where his team members were shrinking in the distance.

Ryan followed my eyes and sighed. "Er, I guess I better get back to my super important job of protecting you ladies from danger." He gave us a mock salute and jogged after his buddies.

"Um," Cherilynn said as she watched him go. "Amélie—"

"If you want him, you can have him," I said.

"Yes, please."

I laughed. "You won't get competition from me, but I can't promise you won't have a mountain of other girls to climb over to get to him."

"Yeah, he's cute."

"Plus, he's a professional singer—he had his own country boy band."

"No way." Cherilynn groaned. "Too perfect. Good voice?"

"Oh yeah. But it's his guitar playing that I love." I dropped my voice to a whisper. "Plus—once—he kissed me. Like, a real kiss."

"Shut up! You passed Ryan up for your boyfriend? This guy of yours must really be something."

I just smiled.

The next day, as we walked alongside some abandoned buildings that had once served as a truck weigh station, several men on horseback galloped past, riding up our flank from behind us. One had an air horn of some kind, and periodically, he gave it three blasts in quick succession, cutting through the din.

Dad looked up from the handcart's crossbar. His eyes blazed. "Quickly, everyone, move to the side of the road." He pushed the handcart to the side and laid the crossbar on the ground so the end of the cart rose up. The cargo was tightly packed, so it didn't shift. He hurried to the back of the cart and reached in, pulling out his rifle.

"What's happening?" I shouted over the uproar the air horn had provoked. Mom hooked her arm through mine and pulled me toward the edge of the road, but her eyes carried the same question.

"Hurry." Dad shooed us like a flock of chickens. "Get behind the cart."

I grasped his arm. "What does that signal mean?"

Dad's face went still and grim. He pressed his lips together.

"Come on, Dad," I said. "We can be strong. But we can be stronger if we know what's going on."

"It means we may be under attack," he said. He handed the other gun, the handgun, to Jarron. Jarron's face flushed. Fear lit his eyes, but then a new intensity took its place.

Dad looked him square in the face. "Tuck it away. If you hear one long blast on the air horn, everyone immediately lie down on the ground behind the cart. You too, Jarron."

I felt a sick shock spread over me.

Dad stood in front of the cart, holding the rifle across his arms.

Other men—many others—did the same. All around us, a sea of former lawyers, accountants, teachers, and businessmen, now grim-faced brothers, clutched hunting rifles and shotguns.

Attack? What did that mean? How big was the attacking force? Was it the Ogden government? Did they have artillery? What about the Legion? A hundred questions zoomed through my mind.

I looked at Mom. She stood still, her face a mask of calm, but her fingers tapped the sides of her legs, fluttering like hummingbirds.

We'd been traveling a divided highway, cutting through a canyon. We spilled all over both the divided right and left lanes, though a gully kept most people from walking in the median. To our left were train tracks, and a narrow road was left of that, hugging the canyon wall. People didn't generally walk on the train tracks since the carts couldn't roll there. The bulk of the group stayed on the main roadway.

A rumble began from the back of the group, getting louder as it came closer. I didn't want to acknowledge what it sounded like.

Tanks.

Twelve tanks rolled down the little road to the left. The mere sight of them—their bulky heaviness, their huge guns—gave me a tight feeling in my gut. We'd known that the so-called government wanted to stop us from taking our vehicles and supplies out of the state, but it'd been long enough now that I'd assumed they'd decided to just let us go. Apparently not. What would happen?

I'd never seen a tank in real life before. They looked impenetrable, unstoppable. I wondered how the military had gotten them running.

Surely they wouldn't use tanks against us. Surely they only meant to intimidate us.

That was working well.

The tanks didn't stop. They kept rolling—I assumed toward the front of the group, where the leaders were. Maybe even the prophet; although perhaps he was already in Missouri.

Men from the Legion—maybe a hundred or so—started forming up in the tanks' path. They drew their weapons. Some of the men dropped to one knee in front, others stood. The tanks' pace didn't change. The men didn't fire as the tanks closed, perhaps because they knew it was pointless.

My stomach clenched. The whole of the Legion wasn't in one place anymore—it was spread throughout the length of the main group, in small companies guarding our flanks. Ryan's little company had been in this area yesterday. Was he one of the men in front of the tanks now? My heart pounded as I stared at the scene.

The men waited until the last moment, but when it became obvious that the tanks wouldn't stop—would roll right over them—they finally scattered to the sides. The tanks moved forward, soon obscured from my view by a bend in the road.

I looked at Dad. His face was covered in grim consternation, and the veins in his hands stood out in stiff ropes as he clutched the rifle. Still, when he glanced at me, he gave me a tight-lipped smile.

"It's going to be all right," he said. "Have faith."

"You want to be up front, don't you?" I asked him.

"Only because I want information in order to know how to best protect you. Don't worry. I'm not going anywhere. At least not yet."

What did he mean by that? I didn't want to think about him leaving us alone again.

The worst part was the waiting. We milled around our handcarts for hours, wondering what was up with the tanks. We heard no sound of gunfire. Noon came and went. People circulated amongst themselves, talking in serious voices, but no one moved their carts from the roadsides.

At last we heard the air horn again, giving four blasts.

"That means the tent captains are to go to the main stake wagon for news," Dad said. Taking his rifle, he hurried away, clearly glad to be able to do something, anything.

After an agonizing half hour, he came back. "Everyone!" he shouted so those nearby could hear. "Go ahead and roll forward, and you'll be told what to do."

"Is it safe?" someone asked.

"As safe as it's going to get."

Dad got behind the crossbar of the handcart, and Jarron ducked in too. I walked next to them. "What's going on, Dad?"

"The military is taking our gas vehicles," Dad growled.

"What? They're taking them? We're just going to let them?"

Dad threw himself against the bar, and the handcart lurched back onto the roadway. "We don't have much choice unless we want to be fired on. The leaders have decided not to go that way. Sure, there's teo hundred thousand of us, but the leaders don't want to send us against big artillery. Too much loss."

I hurried to walk alongside. "But—but—what's going to happen? How can we possibly make it without those vehicles?"

"I won't lie. It's going to be ridiculously hard. Everyone is going to have to take a lot more stuff on their handcarts. Even dividing it between this many people, the loads are going to be overwhelming."

"What happened at the front?" Jarron asked.

"You'll see."

I dragged my feet forward step by step, feeling a curious mixture of dread and anticipation. My eyes searched ahead for a hint, but I almost was afraid to look. What would I see? My stomach churned with nervousness and worry. I prayed I wouldn't witness any dead bodies or precious things rolled flat by tanks.

It took an hour for us to reach where the front of the group had been. There we saw all our vehicles lined up—hundreds of them—from semitrucks to smaller pickups like the Bluebird. Men directed each family to bring their handcart up to one of the trucks, where more supplies were then added to their original load. Members of the Nauvoo Legion stood with rifles at the ready, standing guard over the people transferring supplies out of the vehicles. I wished they could have driven off the attackers, but logically, I knew that didn't make sense. Rifles against tanks?

The tanks were spaced across the roadways, blocking the path. They'd been positioned so that a handcart or small horse-drawn wagon could pass between, but nothing larger. The spot had been carefully chosen—the canyon walls prevented any idea of going around to the sides.

Maybe our little militia wasn't enough to go up against tanks, or, like Dad said, the leaders felt there would be too much loss. Still, the unfairness of it burned my gut. I'd thought that's why we had a militia—in case of an attack like this.

Frustration welled up inside me. Since there were so many people in front of us, I could see that many carts and small wagons had moved beyond the roadblock already, going between the tanks. There wouldn't be enough room to fit the vehicles' remaining supplies on the carts left to load. Not even close. And that was saying nothing about the big gasoline and water tankers, the mobile hospital, the trucks carrying people who couldn't walk.

I wasn't the only one feeling scared. All around me, people were freaking out. Lots of women and kids were crying. Most of the men looked determined, and not just a few looked emotional. I saw Cherilynn with her arm around her mom, both looking like they were about to fall apart.

I swallowed as our cart rolled up to one of the trucks. I looked at Dad, with his worried, exhausted face. Mom, eyebrows drawn, lips set in a line. Jarron and Ethan with their long skinny arms, which would have to pull and pull and push and push, nearly all day, every day but Sunday.

We'd all have to reach down deep and get tough.

I listened as leaders told people they'd have to leave some of their belongings on the side of the road. Most people didn't have much, but nearly everyone had a few things, precious things. We didn't since we'd already left everything behind, but we were the exception. I saw a few try to stuff things into backpacks or carry them in their arms. I could tell that for some, this was the moment when the trek became real.

And for some, it was the moment the trek ended. They turned their carts around and left.

We rearranged our cart a little, but mostly they just piled sacks and boxes of food on top of our stuff. Our cart—once one of the lighter ones—now nearly disappeared under the bulk of its burden.

When we finished, Dad pulled us all together into a family hug, his arms strong around us. "We can do this. I know we can," he said. "But we can't do it without God's help."

Then he bowed his head, and with his arms still encircling us, he prayed. It was more a priesthood blessing on the whole family—something beyond a usual prayer. I felt the Spirit wash over me, and for a few moments, no one could speak. Then we said our amens, but the prayer/blessing felt like it was still open-ended, still feeding us strength.

"Okay, let's do it," Jarron said. He and Dad stood within the crossbar, put their hands on it, and pushed. The cart inched forward. I watched the muscles in their arms strain against the weight.

"Come on, Mom, Ethan," I said, walking to the back of the cart and hooking my cane over its edge. The three of us pushed, and the cart rolled forward. I wouldn't be able to push long, but I could for a moment or two.

We all whooped and hollered a bit, and I felt a surge of pride and happiness in the simple joy of being a Hatch. Then I remembered where we had to go.

Right between the tanks.

The tanks sat silent—plenty scary even without their motors rumbling. I had no idea if they could shoot their guns with the motors off, but I supposed they shut them down to conserve fuel. To act as a barrier for our vehicles, they didn't need to do anything but sit there.

A couple of soldiers with stoic expressions sat on top of each, and perhaps there were more men inside. I couldn't tell. They held weapons but only watched as people passed through the gaps. It was hard to see from where I walked, but it looked like they had the same weird marking on their temples that we'd seen on the soldiers in Salt Lake City.

I felt totally creeped out pushing our cart between the tanks—two gargantuan hulks of steel. I tried to blank my mind of the fear that threatened to paralyze me. Logically, I knew that thousands of people had already passed safely and there was no reason to think the tanks would suddenly decide to start shooting or squishing people. Still, I hated every step it took to walk between and out the other side.

I looked over my shoulder as we slowly continued. Fear lessened. Anger took its place. How dare they take our stuff?

CHAPTER EIGHT

Zack

WE RODE THROUGH MORE EMPTY country, giving roads a wide berth.
We had good coats, but I never felt warm anymore. Just cold. All the
time. The worst was if the wind kicked up. We'd bury our heads under
hats and scarves, turn our collars up, and hunch over our saddles.

Often we crossed fields of dead crops, our horses rustling through
unharvested grain. I thought about the group of people we'd fended
off, and I wondered if they'd found any food yet. It made me sad to
think about how many hungry people there had to be in the country
right now with all this food lying there shriveling. There was no good
way to get it to them, and hardly anyone knew these days how to turn
hard wheat kernels or pods of dry beans into something that resembled
food. I mean, you couldn't exactly throw it in the microwave and
expect to get any good out of it—even if microwaves worked. I sighed.
So much had changed.

That evening, we made camp in an abandoned tractor shed, the
rusting hulks of old farm machinery looming around us. It was still
bone-cold inside, but at least our shelter kept the wind off.

"If I'm reading the map right, we should hit our next supply stop
about noon tomorrow," I said.

"Five days in a row of roughing it is plenty," Christian said. "I
wonder what the supply stop will be like."

"We shouldn't get our hopes up on it being like Hyrum and Annie's
place." But anything would be a welcome change from curling up on

the hard, cold ground. And the variety in our food packs had seriously dwindled, so a restocking would be welcome. Soup packets kept us alive but left us craving a change.

In the morning, we departed the scant protection of the tractor shed, cutting through a field of yellow stubble toward the little back road the map specified. The road scissored around farms, but as long as I could keep its guidance in my sights, we took a more direct path.

"So, Trey, the Rangers . . . Did you get deployed, then?" I asked.

"Yeah, Afghanistan, six-month tour."

"Whoa," Christian said.

"What were your duties?" I asked.

"They had us all over the place, but mostly I worked as a sniper, covering our guys as they moved in on different targets."

"So I guess you had to kill a lot of people."

"Daily."

The memory of shooting the man in Dad's pickup swam over me. I felt the same hard clench in my gut I always got. The only way I'd managed to deal with the memory was to simply shut it out, but every time I turned around, something came up to remind me of what I was constantly trying to forget.

"Does it get easier?" I asked.

"Killing people?" He turned and gave me a searching look. "Hey, if you're worried you'll have to kill someone on this journey, just remember—that's why I'm here. Hopefully I'll be able to save you from having to take on that burden."

Christian said something about how amazing Trey was to do that for us while I tried to pull myself together.

"Hey, are you okay?" Trey asked.

"Yeah, I'm fine. It's just that a few months back, I shot this guy. He killed my dad and was taking off in our truck, and—it just sort of happened." I paused to take a deep breath. "I'm definitely not used to it."

"That's rough, bro," Christian said. "Sorry about your dad. Is your mom doing okay?"

"She died when I was little."

"So you're—"

"Alone." I broke in. Which was pretty much the truth, except for Lee. And God.

We fell silent and rode the rest of the day without trouble. As twilight started to gather, I was surprised to see a couple of figures outlined on the ridgeline. Apparently these people didn't care who saw them. They rode directly toward us.

"What now?" Trey said. "I'm not in the mood to make any deals."

We got our rifles out just to have them handy. Trey leveled his at the approaching pair and watched them through the scope. I felt myself relax a smidgeon. I knew if Trey felt he should, he could easily pick these guys off. One, two.

I raised my binoculars. Just as I thought—two men on horseback. A scan of the horizon showed no others. When they got about a hundred yards off, they slowed to a walk and rode forward with their hands held up.

"We don't want trouble," one shouted. "We have information."

"From who?" I shouted back as we edged closer.

"From the Church people. About your next supply stop."

That definitely caught my interest. Either these people had authentic information for us, or they knew a whole lot about who we were and what we were doing out here. Either way, we'd need to talk.

"I'm Ferrell, and that's Beak," the rider on the left said, a tall but broad man with a scattering of dark hair but only on his chin. Beak— shorter and stocky with an impressive nose—nodded to us.

"You say you have information for us. How do you know who we are? How did you know where to find us?" I asked.

"The Church people received a message via ham radio," Ferrell explained, "and we're part of the network. The leaders needed to get a message to you, and we're the closest on the network to where they thought you'd be. It did take us a while to find you."

"How do I know you are who you say you are?" I asked.

Ferrell shrugged. "I guess you can take our message or leave it."

"Okay. Hand it over."

He took a folded square of paper from his jacket pocket. I nudged Big Black close enough that I could reach out and take it, feeling Trey's careful eye on the two strangers.

To: Daniel Foreman
From: Gilbert Reeves, Commander, Main Company

For Immediate Transmittal via Secure Ham Network

URGENT AND CONFIDENTIAL

Bro. Foreman,

When the overland team reaches your supply stop please relay the following to its captain, Zack Allman:

On November 1, the cavalry unit was attacked. The enemy forces were highly organized and well equipped. Under cover of darkness, the sentries were overwhelmed, and the unit came under fire. Miraculously, none were killed, although they suffered heavy casualties. Many were taken prisoner.

The cargo was lost to enemy forces.

We believe the attack was coordinated under the direction of the Southern Quadrant's command, but this is not confirmed.

With this loss, the overland team's mission becomes even more critical. Please make them aware that we believe there is a security breach within our ranks. The various units' movements appear to be anticipated, and he should assume that his route and planned stops are known to the enemy forces.

Any transmittal of information should be considered no longer secure at this time. We are taking steps to restore communication privacy.

Please inform if and when the supply stop takes place and if this communication is received by Bro. Allman.

Gilbert Reeves, Commander
Main Company
Transcribed by Sgt. Richard Rupp

The news about the cavalry unit swept over me in a black fog. I couldn't internalize what it meant, not yet.

I knew keeping the contents of the memo secret from Trey and Christian would be super awkward, but if I let them read it, they'd know I hadn't been completely open with them. They'd know we weren't just a decoy. I looked at each of them, searching their faces. I sent up a little prayer to be sure, but I knew. Despite the captain telling me to keep my secrets, I knew it was time to share my load with Trey and Christian, that I could trust them completely.

Swallowing hard, I handed the paper to Christian. "It looks like this was supposed to be given to me at the next supply stop." He read it and passed it to Trey.

Ferrell said, "Yes. It was sent there first. But that location isn't secure anymore. So they forwarded us the message, and it's our privilege to bring it to you, sir."

Something in his voice, a strange fervor, made me look at him in surprise. His eyes burned with passion.

Beak said, "We've been searching for you since yesterday. Glad to finally find you. Luckily, their descriptions of you guys are dead on. You look exactly like they said you would."

I squirmed a bit at that. Maybe it should have made me feel more confident that these guys were who they said they were, but it mostly creeped me out. "Okay, well, thanks for bringing the message. I appreciate the effort and time." Thoughts rushed through my mind. I wanted to talk to Christian and Trey about what had happened to the cavalry unit and the fact that there would be no supply stop tomorrow.

And even more nerve-twiddling, I knew the time had come to talk to Trey and Christian about the little pouch in my pocket. I felt a zing of anxiousness. I hoped they'd understand why I'd kept that from them.

I didn't want to brush these messengers off after their long search, but I needed to get to it. "If you talk to the headquarters people again, tell them thanks." I reined Big Black to step around.

Before I could move away, Ferrell raised his hand. "Hey, we'd like to travel with you guys for a bit," he burst out. "I mean, it would be our honor. We could help with turns at watch and stuff."

"Thanks, but I'm sure you have a lot of important things to get back to."

"Nothing is more important than this," Beak said. "Not remotely."

I glanced at Trey and lifted an eyebrow.

Trey said, "We'll pass. Thanks though."

"But we can help get you through this area. We know it real well. We can help hook you up with some supplies if you need, too," Farrell said.

I scratched my head. "Well . . ." We would need food very soon, and if tomorrow's supply stop was unusable, we'd need another source.

"It would mean a lot to us," Ferrell said eagerly. "We want to help the cause. We're going your direction. We have the same goals."

"We do need supplies," I said slowly. Finally, making up my mind, I answered. "We can camp together for the night. Tomorrow we'll see about restocking."

We found a gully with a few scrabbly trees and pitched our tents. As we heated up the tiresome soup of the day, it was nice to see Ferrell and Beak pull out some bread to share.

Ferrell grinned. "You don't know how exciting this is for us."

"Exciting?" Christian snorted. "Sitting out in the middle of nowhere, eating chicken noodle soup?"

"Just the chance to help with the end-times preparations. What a privilege," Ferrell said. "You guys are so lucky. You're making history."

I wrinkled my nose. "We're just doing our little part. It's not a big deal."

"You're far too modest. I bet some of the Book of Mormon people thought the same thing at the time, and look what giants they are to us now. Think of Ammon, for example."

I'd only read the Book of Mormon once, and I didn't remember a lot, but I did remember that amazing story. I'd never thought about Ammon as a guy like me, just trying to do his best in difficult times. The thought rocked me back.

"Someday people are going to read about your accomplishments," Ferrell continued. "You'll be an inspiration to them. I'd give anything to be in a position to do that. Beak and me, well, we've been working in the background in whatever way we can, and when we got assigned to come out here and deliver your message, we couldn't have been more pleased."

Beak shifted forward. "For years now, people have been dreaming dreams—visions—of the Saints getting called to leave their homes and everything behind and go live in tent cities. We're literally watching this come to pass, and if you think about it, it really is exciting. You guys are out here like Porter Rockwell, getting the job done."

"Who?" I looked at Trey. He shrugged.

"You don't know who Porter Rockwell is?" Ferrell looked amazed.

"No. Should I?"

"Oh, man, he was one awesome guy," Ferrell said. "Lived back in Joseph Smith's time. He was Joseph's bodyguard for a while, and he didn't let anything get in the way of doing what needed to be done."

Christian smiled. "Kind of a weird one though, right? Like a crazy mountain-man type."

Ferrell shook his head. "Say what you will. He didn't let irrelevant rules or traditions keep him from his righteous goals. My ultimate hero."

I didn't consider myself uptight about rules and such, but the fact Ferrell practically worshipped this Porter Rockwell guy gave me pause. It said a lot about Ferrell, I thought.

When we'd finished eating and cleaning up, I motioned to Trey and Christian to follow me a ways away from camp. The other two watched with fervent interest as we walked off.

"Kind of an odd situation," I began when I knew we couldn't be overheard. "These guys seem sort of harmless, and maybe they can help us with our supply situation. But before we talk about that, how about that message? I'm blown away. I don't know what to think."

Christian shook his head. "I know; I feel the same. Just thinking about those guys we trained with, lived with, coming under attack. And many of them taken prisoner? Whoa. Amazing no one was killed."

Trey said, "We all knew this could happen. Actually, if you think about it, it was pretty much a sure bet they'd get attacked."

"It's so weird that they're out of the picture now. So weird," I said, gathering up my courage.

I took a deep breath. "There's something I need to tell you guys. You're probably wondering why the message says that our mission is more important than ever now. Why would we need to continue being a decoy for a group that's been taken out."

Trey folded his arms across his chest, that mysterious smile teasing the corners of his mouth.

"Does seem odd, bro," Christian said.

"You know the decoy package on the back of my horse—the Bible?" I said. "It really is just a Bible. But I do have something else." I reached into my jacket pocket and pulled out the little pouch, the one I'd kept close and unseen all this time. "I think it's time for us to be on the same page." I tugged the drawstrings loose and pulled out the little vacuum-packed bag of seeds, the vial of brownish liquid, and the plastic case holding the tiny memory card, cupping all three in my hands.

"I know you can't see these things very well since it's dark, but what we've got here are items that will allow the Church to recreate whatever was taken from the cavalry unit. I don't know the details."

I searched their faces as best I could in the dark, hoping they wouldn't feel slighted about me holding this information back from them for so long. But even though I'd been told to keep it to myself, I felt sure it was right to share it with them now.

What if I was just finding out that Christian or Trey had kept a secret like this from me? I might be miffed.

Maybe they were keeping secrets.

"Smart to send it two different ways—with us and with the main cavalry unit—to increase its chances of getting through," Christian said.

"Yup," Trey said.

Their voices seemed calm, not angry. I decided to plunge on. "It looks like our plans will need to change now the cavalry unit is out and our route isn't so secret anymore. I guess we won't be eating steaks tomorrow night at a supply stop."

"I'd say we shouldn't plan on being able to make *any* of our stops," Trey said.

I tried to swallow the panic bubbling up inside. "Then what do we do?"

"Let these guys help us resupply once, and then we need to shake them loose," Trey said. "We need to go even more covert, and we can't do that with them hanging on. If you agree."

I nodded. That made sense.

"After that, I've got some ideas for getting food," Christian said. "They used to call me Crazy Boy Scout for a reason." He laughed.

"Okay, let's hit the sack and worry about this tomorrow." I tucked the items back inside the pouch and slipped them into my jacket pocket.

"One more quick thing," Trey said. "Just so you know. Now that we know what you're carrying, our first priority just changed slightly. Now even more, it's all about you. Or more precisely, your pocket contents.

My duty is to do anything and everything I can to make sure the cargo makes it through."

Christian nodded his agreement. I swallowed a huge lump of nerves.

"Thanks, guys," I said. That was so very completely inadequate, but I couldn't say more. We went back to the camp and set up a watch schedule that didn't include our guests. I pointedly ignored Ferrell and Beak's questioning looks and rolled into my blankets.

—+—

The next morning, we got packed up and saddled. I patted Big Black's neck before climbing on. "Looks like we'll be spending some time together after all," I said. He tossed his noble head.

I turned in the saddle toward Ferrell and Beak. "I do appreciate your offer of supplies. Can we head that way now?"

"Sure," Ferrell said.

We traveled roughly east, in the same direction we'd gone the day before, riding through more dead fields. A country road crossed our path, and Ferrell turned left onto it. After a few minutes, a farmhouse and some outbuildings came into view. We headed straight in that direction, following Ferrell and Beak.

"Nice looking place," I said. "This your family's farm?"

"No. Never been here before," Ferrell said without looking at me.

"You know these people?"

"Nope."

"I feel weird about this," I said. "I didn't know you were taking us to just some random farm. The people here won't be expecting to load up a bunch of strangers with their food. I don't want to take anyone's last crumb."

"Your mission is more important."

"What if they don't see it that way? They probably aren't even members of the Church," Christian said.

Ferrell smiled, his eyes glinting. "That's the only thing I know about them. They aren't members. Even more reason to relieve them of some stuff."

"Wait, what? Relieve them?" Christian said, his ruddy face turning redder. "This is your plan? To go in and take stuff by force?"

"We're on the Lord's errand. Nothing else matters."

Christian dug his heels into his horse's sides, getting out in front of everyone. He spun, forcing Ferrell to stop. We all pulled up, me next to Ferrell. "We're not doing this," Christian said hotly. "I'm not going to go pillage someone's farm."

"Then get out of the way," Ferrell shouted, suddenly aflame. "Your heart isn't in the right place. You don't deserve to be in this company if you aren't prepared to do what needs doing."

I opened my mouth, but Christian cut me off. "You're out of line." He jabbed a finger at Ferrell.

"Let us pass," Ferrell said. "You're the one obstructing the mission. It's up to me to stop you." To my horror, he drew a handgun.

"What do you think you're doing?" I shouted.

"Getting you supplies." He leveled the gun at Christian.

"Are you insane?" I lurched sideways in my saddle, flinging my hand out to knock the gun away.

The gun went off with an earsplitting bang. Blood bloomed on Christian's left thigh, and he cried out, hunching forward. His horse reared, and Christian fell hard into a patch of slushy mud.

Big Black startled at the gunshot but settled enough for me to leap off my saddle and grab Nutmeg's reins so he wouldn't trample his poor rider.

"Oh no, oh no," Ferrell cried.

Before I knew what happened, Trey had Ferrell's gun in his own hand, aimed at Ferrell, and his own gun in the other hand, trained on Beak.

"Get off your horses and sit on the ground," Trey said, his voice flat and emotionless. I bent over Christian, who groaned and clutched his muddy, blood-splattered leg.

They hurried to obey. "Didn't mean to shoot him," Ferrell said, obviously shaken. He looked like he was about to cry. "Please, I'm sorry."

Trey pulled a length of rope from his saddlebag and, with a few deft motions, tied Ferrell and Beak's hands behind their backs. They submitted without protest. Ferrell looked like he was about to throw up.

"What are you going to do to us?" Beak asked.

"Not as much as you deserve." Trey hobbled their horses nearby. "You'll work your hands loose eventually but not before we're long away from you idiots."

"I'm sorry," Ferrell said. "We only wanted to help."

"Just shut up," Trey said. He walked over to me and Christian.

I had to admit I didn't know much about doctoring, so I was glad to have Trey's help. It seemed the bullet had passed right through the side of Christian's thigh—grazing his horse's hip as it exited—so there were two wounds, in and out. Christian lay on his back, gray-faced and grim while Trey and I applied pressure.

"You're lucky," Trey said. "Didn't hit an artery." We cleaned and bandaged it as best we could, tied a T-shirt tightly around the whole of it, and got him back up on his horse. A painful sequence of movements, but Christian bore it well.

"You okay to ride?" I asked.

"Let's get out of here." Christian looked pale but forced a grin. "I'm good. Just promise me one thing."

"What's that?"

"That I'll get a cool scar."

CHAPTER NINE

Amélie

WE TRAVELED UP THE CLIMBING road until about five o'clock, when
the group halted for the night. I felt awful for Dad. He looked so tired.

"Are you okay?" I asked him as we pulled our cart next to the tent
wagon.

"I'm fine." He smiled at me and squeezed my shoulder. "How are
you doing?"

I smiled back. "I'm good." My leg hurt as usual, but no way was I
going to complain. Not to him.

Dad wasn't even close to done for the night. He still had to be in
charge of setting up our campsite for the twenty of us. The four other
dads would help, of course, but I guessed they'd be even more worn out,
since they were possibly not used to the physical labor Dad was. In any
case, none of them had arrived yet, and Dad wasn't likely to sit around
waiting for them to show up. He'd just do it himself.

Luckily, he hadn't been put on the water-fetching team today. Now
that we didn't have the water tankers anymore, each stake had to send a
wagon to the river for water each night—a time-consuming and tiring
process.

Mom and I scrounged in the wagon for the night's food bag—more
difficult than usual since the tent wagon had also received an extra
measure of supplies to carry and things were a bit buried. Then the first
chore was to get a fire going to boil water. We needed to boil enough
water to refill the water buckets on each handcart for the coming day,
and that took time.

Next, we started getting the ingredients ready for the soup pot. As I opened cans, I noticed Cherilynn and her mom come into camp. They looked pretty haggard.

I walked over. "Are you guys doing all right? Can I get you some water or something?"

"No, but thanks," Cherilynn said. Her mom sat down on the ground and didn't look up from the veil of hair hanging over her eyes. "Sorry we're late. We'll be over to help with dinner in a sec."

"Where's your dad?"

"He'll be right here." She leaned close and whispered, "They've been fighting again."

"Again?"

"Haven't you noticed? I mean, they used to fight a lot at home, but now? Good grief." Cherilynn's face looked sad and worried.

"They're probably just tired," I said. "We all are. It's hard to stay cheery."

"I never see your folks fighting."

True. Mom and Dad didn't fight. Never had, at least not when I could hear. It just wasn't their way.

I shrugged. "Hard times bring out the best in some people. Others, not so much. It'll be okay." I put my hand on her elbow.

Cherilynn smiled with one of those overbright grins people use when they're worried or embarrassed but want to drop the subject. "After we eat, wanna work on the project?"

I shook my head. "Let's take the night off. It's been an insane day. Besides, Dad says there's going to be a burial tonight."

"A burial? For who?"

"An older person in the stake, a Brother Jones. Dad says they'll have a memorial on Sunday. I didn't know this, but apparently a few people from the whole group die every day. Each stake handles their own services. This is the first one for our stake though."

Cherilynn's face drooped. "Every day. Huh. I guess that would happen, no matter if we were on the road or not."

"Yeah. And every day babies are born too."

"Seriously?"

I nodded. "On our first trek, there was just one birth, which I got to help with. Hard. But incredible. My mom helps with babies all the time now."

Cherilynn shook her head. "Not the way I'd picture having a baby."

The soup cooked over a fire made from the random brush and scrub oak gathered by Janny and a couple of the other preteens in our group. Each handcart carried several five-gallon tanks of propane, but they were to be carefully conserved for days when there'd be nothing to burn.

I massaged my aching leg. I tried not to be gloomy, but the whole thing with the army tanks made it hard. I couldn't let myself think about how far we had to go, and we'd only just begun.

-+-

After dinner Mom and I walked to the grave site for Brother Jones, which was about a hundred yards off the right side of the road. I managed the rough, uneven ground only with heavy reliance on my cane—and Mom. Only a few people, mostly Brother Jones's family, gathered at the grave, dug the hour before by a team of stake brethren. The coffin was a simple wooden box, which they lowered into the ground with ropes. I wondered where they'd gotten the wood to build it. Maybe one of the wagons was stacked with pine planks for coffins. I didn't know. The Church had thought of everything, it seemed.

It sobered me to think that three or four others in the big group had probably died that day and other graves had been made—that our path would be dotted with graves the entire way to Missouri.

After dedicating the grave, the stake men shoveled dirt in to fill it, setting in a wooden marker carved with Brother Jones's name. In the morning we'd leave the grave behind. The likelihood of anyone putting flowers there—ever—was pretty remote. The thought made me sad, but I reminded myself that only his mortal remains lay in that spot. His spirit was free.

I thought about Brother Jones, who I'd never met. He must have been amazing. Only days from death, he'd resolved to be part of this trek. Of course, he didn't know exactly when he'd die, but he'd been quite old. I'm sure it would have been much easier for him to stay behind and sleep his last few nights in his own soft bed. Instead, he'd come with us, braving the cold nights and long days of walking. When it came to getting tough, Brother Jones had it all. Could I be as faithful?

-+-

Over the next few days, Cherilynn and I built up quite a stash of bike-riding (and walking) helpers for the project. Little by little, my notebook filled up with names. I had to smile at many of the interests people listed. Computers. Marching band. Softball. Ballet. Hardly any of them had a part in our new, strange world. The leaders who used this information would have their work cut out for them when it came to distilling it for their use. Maybe the people interested in computers could somehow help in getting power back once we got to Missouri. Maybe the girl who used to be the captain of her softball team could be tapped for her leadership skills. And so on. But figuring all that out would be someone else's job. Mine was just to gather the information and then turn it over to the leaders. That thing about being the "liaison" had no meaning for me yet.

"I'm sure you could do the project faster without me," I said to Cherilynn one day.

"What are you talking about?"

"Just that I'm slow. You know."

"No, I don't."

I stared at her. Of course she knew I was slow. Every time we were together, she'd have my slowness shoved in her face. My limp. My cane. She had to wait for me all the time. I wiggled my cane at her. "Lee the Cripple Girl," I said.

"Oh, that," she said. "Actually, I hardly notice it."

That pretty much blew my mind. "You're kidding, right?" The limp defined me, at least in my own mind. I'd tried to move beyond it, and after the first trek, I did feel I'd made progress. But it was hard to not let my limitations dominate my thinking, especially now that my days were filled with physical effort. It was hard to accept the idea that others didn't categorize me as *broken*. Sometimes that label seemed as enormous as a billboard, complete with flashing lights.

"No, I'm serious," Cherilynn said. "Of course it wouldn't be faster without you. You're the main person. I'm just glad to help out. What happened, anyway? Did you sprain your ankle?"

Wow.

She didn't even know this was a lifelong disability. She'd assumed that in a week or two I'd be good as new. If only.

"My leg got run over by our truck when I was little." I kept my expression smooth. "It got crushed pretty good."

"Ohhhh. Gosh. I'm sorry. They can't fix it?"

"No, they've tried. Surgeries galore. It is what it is."

"Wow, that really stinks. But it explains a lot."

"What do you mean?"

"Why you're so tough and cool."

I laughed self-consciously, but I felt pleased she'd said that and that she didn't seem to think of me as fragile or overly weird. As a matter of fact, she went straight from that into planning our next night's work on the project. Like the thing with my leg didn't affect her relationship with me in the slightest.

How I loved that.

-+-

That night in camp, Cherilynn's parents got into it again. Over the last few days, the arguing had settled into chilly glares and only the bare minimum of conversation. But now the shouting resumed with Cherilynn sitting nearby on a log, her head down on her knees. I sat beside her, but she didn't move. Neither of us spoke.

Across the campfire, things heated up. "If I wasn't trapped here, I'd be so gone."

"Nothing's stopping you."

"Witch."

"Jerk."

On and on they went. The rest of our tent group tried to endure it, hoping they'd run out of steam soon. It wasn't like there was somewhere else to go.

Finally, Dad said, "You guys need to cool it."

"You need to shut up," Cherilynn's dad said, jabbing Dad in the chest with a stiff finger.

Cherilynn jumped up. "Just stop it," she cried. "Just stop."

"Butt out, Cherilynn," her dad snapped over her mom's shouts. "This isn't your business."

"Except that when you guys fight like this, my a-fib goes nuts," Cherilynn said, sinking back to her log seat.

Both parents fell silent.

"Are you okay?" I whispered.

"Dizzy."

Her mom came over. "Okay, Cherie, do the clench."

"Don't you think I tried?"

"Do it again."

Beside me, I saw Cherilynn draw a deep breath and then clench the muscles in her stomach and chest.

"Did it work?"

"Yeah." Cherilynn got up from the log and went into the tent. I followed her.

"Were you telling the truth? Is it better?"

Cherilynn sprawled on her sleeping bag. "Sort of."

"What does it feel like?"

"Pounding. Racing. Like a fish flopping around in my chest."

"But your medicine—"

"It helps most of the time, but being stressed sometimes makes it worse. Or if I'm scared."

"Are you scared?"

She paused. "That fighting makes me stressed out." She flung an arm across her eyes. "Sorry. It's sort of hard to talk. I can't think straight."

I squeezed her arm then slipped from the tent. Being stressed or scared? Sounded a lot like our whole trip.

─┼─

About ten days after the military took our vehicles, Dad came home from a stake meeting with an announcement for our tent group.

"The stake is holding a thank-you party for the Nauvoo Legion tomorrow night," he said as we gathered for evening prayers.

I wrinkled my nose. "Why? I mean, I'm thankful they're here with us, but why now? You know, right after we had our stuff taken from us and they weren't able to do a thing about it."

Dad smiled. "Yeah, I can see how you'd feel that way. But you'll understand better tomorrow."

"Wait . . . All two thousand of them? That's the same number as the stake itself."

"They're splitting up among the stakes, so we'll have twenty as our special guests."

On the first trek, we'd gathered as a stake quite often since we all ate together. Now we had church together on Sundays, but we ate with our tent groups. A party? I wondered what that would consist of, but it was something different to look forward to. With the endless sameness of each day, I welcomed it.

The next evening after dinner, we walked over to our stake's designated gathering place—a hilly area next to the road. We sat down on the ground. Of course.

President Carroll pulled out his megaphone. He motioned with a hand, and twenty young men in Legion uniforms walked up to stand beside him.

"Brothers and sisters, thanks for coming to the party. I'm glad you weren't already booked for the evening since it was sort of last minute." Everyone chuckled.

"We're going to have music and dancing in a bit, but first there's a story we want everyone to hear." He reached out to one of the soldiers. "This is Taylor Horowitz. He's going to tell you a little about what the Nauvoo Legion has been up to the last week or so."

Everyone clapped. The young man stepped close and took the megaphone, clearing his throat with a nervous little cough. "Hi, every-one," he said. The crowd roared "hi" back, and people laughed, putting him a bit more at ease.

"As you know, we had a frustrating experience when tanks showed up from the Ogden faction. I know it was scary and discouraging for you, and let me tell you, it really was for us guys in the Legion too. We felt helpless. Not having the vehicles makes an already hard trip so much harder. But the leaders thought it through and prayed a lot about it. They felt that we'd be able to get along without the trucks, if only by the skin of our teeth. Actually, there were a lot of extra supplies on those trucks. We'd planned to take them into Missouri to help out once we got there, but the leaders knew we could squeak by without some of those supplies. That's one of the reasons why they decided we shouldn't try to fight back. They knew people would get killed. There was pretty much no avoiding that, and our chances against tanks weren't good.

"But a few days ago, our rear guards discovered the tanks were once again pursuing us. The same twelve tanks plus many of our trucks traveling behind them."

A frightened murmur swept over the crowd. I stared at the young man, fastened to every word.

"We're guessing they took our trucks back to Ogden, unloaded them, and decided to come back for more. They were probably surprised at how many supplies we were able to unload and carry off. They probably figured we were easy pickings, especially since we didn't put up a fight the first time. But this time, things were different. We couldn't let them take more. We're barely going to make it with what we have. So the Legion got creative. We had to act fast.

"You remember how the shape of the canyon helped the tanks the first time. We couldn't go around their blockade. Well, we found a place where we could use that to our advantage. A few days ago, you passed through this spot. Maybe you remember it. The road is bordered by high hills on each side. In one place, a train bridge goes across the road.

"The Legion secreted itself in the hillsides and along the bridge. We let the tanks roll through, and when the trucks came up, we shot their tires out. We also shot into the engines and fuel tanks as much as possible. Those trucks are pretty much unusable now, let me tell you. They had troops that returned fire, but we were hard to hit in our hidden locations. I'm happy to report that although we had a few injuries, no one was killed.

"The tanks turned and came back to assist, but we were long gone, slipping around the sides under cover of night. Without trucks to haul our supplies, the tanks had no purpose. They've returned back down the highway.

"I'm sure we'll still have troubles on the remainder of the trip, but I don't think they'll come from the Ogden faction. We're almost out of their territory. So I believe we're safe from that particular threat now."

I'm not sure how much more the young man was going to say, but the crowd's whistling and cheering cut him off. After a minute or so, he grinned and handed the megaphone back to President Carroll.

Musicians started to play, reminding me all so clearly of our first trek and Ryan with his magic guitar. I wondered which stake had him as their special guest. I was bummed it wasn't ours, but with a hundred stakes, I had to admit the chances that he'd be sent to our stake were pretty small. I wondered if he was playing his guitar for that lucky stake or if he was content to play soldier for now.

It was a little tough to sit and watch the dancing. Everyone looked like they were having a ton of fun, and of course, it reminded me so much of Zack and the way he danced with me during our first trek.

I look at Zack standing beside me. The blessed boy reads my mind.
"Let's get this party started." He holds his hands out to me.
"How?" I whisper.
"Step on my boots and hang on. I'll do the rest."
I lay down my cane.

But I refused to let myself get blue. Instead, a feeling of thankfulness spread over me. We were definitely being watched over. I sat back and soaked the feeling in.

—|—

On September 30, we ran into a group of people from Denver. They'd left the city and headed north, intersecting our route. They'd heard of us. Not sure how, with such limited communications. But apparently the news of two hundred thousand Mormons on the move had spread. We were becoming a legend.

We hadn't noticed anyone joining the group so far, so this was the first time our little group met any add-ins. A middle-aged man named Michael and his brother Brian from the Denver group happened to fall into step beside us.

"What was it like in Denver after the EMP?" Mom asked. "We're farm folks, so we have no idea what it would have been like in a big city."

"You don't want to know," Michael said. "Let's just say that it doesn't take long for people to regress to a beastly state." His eyes got a far-away, glazed look. "I saw things I hope I never see again. You'd be surprised how a little hunger changes people."

A somber quiet fell over the group. "I can't imagine," Mom said. "Especially when faced with trying to feed their kids. People get desperate."

Michael nodded. "I saw some heroic things too. Unfortunately, not nearly enough. And those heroes are pretty much all dead."

Heroes. All dead. I tried not to think of Zack, but I couldn't help it. Zack, my amazing, hunky, completely frustrating, and faraway boyfriend, who had a penchant for jumping in front of bullets. I felt physical pain in my gut and nearly staggered from it.

"What's the city like now?" Dad asked.

"It's weird," Brian said. "Nearly the whole place is deserted. That great big huge city is quiet. Without power, without food, it's not a good place to be. I'm sure there are people still there, in their hidey-holes, but if you were to walk around the city, you'd see no one. And you'd probably get shot for what might be in your pocket. The lucky ones got out of the city early on. The rest either joined gangs or they're dead."

"Is it all bombed out and stuff?" Ethan asked.

"Actually, no. At least not that I saw. You'd think it would have been hit by a nuke, that all the major cities were hit, but Denver apparently wasn't. Info is sketchy, but I don't know of radioactive damage. People say the big cities on the coasts—Seattle, L.A., New York, D.C., and so on, are all gone though. The EMP was all it took to empty Denver. And now I suppose the attackers could waltz right in and take over an unbombed, largely undamaged city and there'd be no one to stop them."

"Who are the attackers?" I said. "Do we even know that? We saw a couple of them in Idaho, on our first trek. They looked Middle Eastern and one had an English accent, but I don't know anything else."

"I heard that it's a group out of the Middle East whose main goal is to take out Israel. Perhaps a coalition of countries. Sort of makes a weird sort of sense, I suppose. Eliminate the US from the picture—neutralize us—and suddenly, tough-boy Israel isn't so tough anymore."

"But would a group like that really have the capability to set off an EMP like this one? They'd need a space program," Dad said.

"Who knows what those guys can do? I bet they made a deal with another country, like China or Russia or someone, for help launching the thing. Maybe they said, 'Hey, China, how about we get together? Isolate Israel and punish the big, bad, evil US at the same time.' Don't be surprised if you see Chinese troops at some point."

Oh great, I thought. Maybe I was better off not knowing that.

—┼—

The days weren't all bad. I relished the time with Dad. I'd gone from missing him—and being angry about it—to being with him 24/7, soaking in his quiet, solid presence. Sometimes I walked beside him while he pushed the cart, talking of random things, keeping him company, anything just to help make it easier for him. Sometimes I watched from behind, where it was oh-so-clear that Dad never complained, never shirked, never stopped trying with everything he had.

Mom seemed to be handling stuff pretty well too. Mom was still Mom though. Even only being able to bring a couple of changes of clothes, she still managed to keep her gypsy chic thing going, and she had her weird granola-hippie habits. Some of her mannerisms never failed to annoy me. But I had to hand it to her. I'd seen her fall apart at the littlest things in the past. Her default mode for dealing with frustration had been to flop down and cry. I'd seen that about a million times. But she hadn't done that at all on this trek. Not once. Where was she getting the strength?

Jarron and Ethan were rock solid too. They seemed to catch the spirit that floated through the group—a spirit of can-do, of rising to the occasion. Not that there were never arguments or that they never got grumpy. Still, I didn't hear them get mad about having to be on the trek. They knew why we were doing this. They got it.

In the past when people around me were all gung-ho, it sometimes made me feel obstinate. But this time, in spite of how corny it sounded, I felt like I understood the pioneers in a small way and why they kept going when it got hard. Of course, now that we had handcarts, the pioneer comparisons were everywhere.

One thing was for sure—when one of those chilly Wyoming winds started howling, I was plenty glad I wasn't feeling *that* blow up my petticoats. Long johns, jeans, woolen socks, and a stout pair of boots were my uniform now. My Chuck Taylors were relegated to my backpack. A few women brought skirts as part of their limited clothing (Mom!), but I rarely saw dresses or bare legs for that matter. I figured the closer we got to October, the more clothing I'd be wearing. Maybe there wouldn't be any left in the handcart at all.

After supper, I limped into the American Fork East Stake camp, clutching my tattered notebook in one hand and my cane in the other. With a practiced eye, I scanned the clumps of tents scattered around the area. People moved around cleaning up dinner and repacking handcarts. I zeroed in on a rail-thin girl who looked maybe fourteen.

"Hi, I'm Amélie," I said, helping her heft a water bucket onto a cart. "I'm working on a survey for the Church. Is it okay if I ask you a couple of questions?"

As I expected, she looked at me quizzically. "What kind of questions?"

"I'm supposed to record all the youths' names and ages and stuff they like to do or are good at," I replied. I'd said these words so many times they rolled right off my tongue, smooth and easy.

"Oh, okay," she said.

I smiled to make her feel a bit more comfortable. People always seemed hesitant at first but usually warmed up with a little encouragement. I took down her name and age. Fourteen. I grinned. To amuse myself, I'd made it a mental game to try and guess people's ages. After all this time, I nearly always got it right.

"So what's your favorite thing to do?" I asked.

She laughed. "Now? Or in real life?"

"Real life."

"Manicures." We both laughed, and I wrote it down.

"Anything else?"

"Facebook." Duly noted.

"What do you think you have a knack for?" I asked.

"I can beat my brother at arm wrestling."

"Sweet. Me too, but don't tell." We talked a little more, and then I popped my pen shut. "That's it. Pretty painless."

She looked a tiny bit disappointed. I recognized the look. I'd seen it a lot because, after all, there's nothing more fun than talking about yourself. It provided the perfect lead-in for me to ask if she'd like to help me go through the rest of the stake, asking the same questions to the other kids. Before I knew it I had a little army of American Fork Beehives and deacons scurrying about with pencils and papers. Once they were done they brought the wad of papers back to me. I stuffed them in the back of my notebook—I'd copy the info later that night—and that was that.

Normally I'd go to the next stake and do it all again. But not this time. Because I was DONE.

I went back to our own tent. I may have looked like a little old lady hobbling along with her cane, but I felt like the conquering hero.

Finished! The project. Done.

I found Cherilynn and gave her a huge victory hug. I even danced a little bit, if you could call it that.

As far as I knew, we'd recorded every single young person in the entire group. My notebook was a battered mess, but it was precious, holding the names, abilities, and talents of thousands of youth from across one hundred stakes. Nearly every single night, I'd gone out with Cherilynn, visiting campsite after campsite. The list of helpers grew, and I spent at least an hour each evening after returning to our tent, copying their gatherings into my notebook. And now it was done. I looked forward to resting in the evenings instead of tromping around on my already tired legs, but I had to admit I'd miss meeting new people. Wow, it'd been hard at first since I'd always been a die-hard introvert, but I'd gotten used to it. Perhaps I couldn't classify myself as "shy" or "reserved" anymore. Weird.

I climbed into my sleeping bag, putting the notebook under my pillow. Tomorrow I'd deliver it to the leaders. I could make the biggest "completed" checkmark of my life.

Maybe I could do important things. Make a difference. Maybe making it through the first trek wasn't just a fluke after all. Maybe I'd actually make it to Missouri in one piece. Maybe they really had picked the right person to run that project. At that moment, I think I felt the least loser-like I ever had.

Good feeling.

+

"Why aren't we packing up?" I asked Dad one morning in October. All around us, other camps were dismantling, but our tent still stood in its place.

"Steel yourself for some hard news. You know Cherilynn has a heart condition."

"Yes." My breath caught.

"She's very sick this morning. Her heart is stuck in a loop of beating hard and fast, and they can't get it to kick out of it, at least so far. Normally, they'd use a defibrillator—that usually works—but we haven't got one, so we're going to stay put for now."

I hurried into our tent. There Cherylinn lay, where I'd left her this morning without a backward glance. Her parents sat beside her, silent for once.

"Cherilynn!" I cried.

"Her heart's racing," her mom said. "It won't stop. It's been like this since yesterday afternoon." She stood and leaned close to whisper in my ear. "The doctor says her heart could give out anytime."

I stared. Now that I thought about it, I hadn't seen Cherilynn at dinner last night. She must have gone straight to bed after we made camp.

Shock spread through my body as I knelt at her side. Cherilynn looked at me, her face full of fear and exhaustion.

"They can't do anything?" I asked. She shook her head.

Her mom said, "Last night, we took her to the medical tent. They've tried it all. Without a defibrillator, clenching all her muscles or coughing are the main alternatives. But she's done that a million times, and it isn't working."

"She's had a blessing?"

"Of course."

I leaned over, putting my face close to hers. Was it really her time to go? No!

"What does it feel like?" I whispered.

"Scary. Weak," she muttered.

"It's okay. It's okay. Just breathe. That's it." I stroked her hair. "Don't think about anything." I tried to broadcast calm instead of the panic that gripped me.

Her face. So pale. I knew that inside her chest, her heart flailed and thrashed. Any moment it might be spent.

I tried to put myself in her situation. I knew Cherilynn's fear was pumping adrenaline through her body and making everything way worse. What would calm her? What had I turned to in my own scary times?

Memories floated forward. Me in the hospital for yet another surgery on my leg. A nurse with an IV needle. Sharp. Sting. Pain. Crying, shaking, scared. And then Mom, rubbing my feet with something warm, smooth, soothing. Her voice soft, singing but almost tuneless. She spread her calm on me like a salve.

First I thought of fetching Mom to come and do this for Cherilynn. But she didn't know Mom very well, and it might be weird. Maybe I could do it.

Then I had a better idea. "Be right back," I said and hobbled as quickly as I could to our handcart, pulling out Mom's bag of herbal concoctions. Returning to the tent, I pulled Cherilynn's mom aside.

"We have to help her not be scared," I whispered. "Even though we're scared to death ourselves. Maybe you can pass some calm along to her."

"How?" She looked so hopeful it nearly broke my heart.

"You give her your peacefulness. My mom used to do that for me. You can do it for Cherilynn."

"But I don't feel peaceful."

"You have to try—for Cherilynn." I reached into Mom's bag and pulled out a handful of little vials of oil. Lavender. Geranium. Bergamot. "Mom rubbed my hands and feet with these. Maybe they helped. But it was mostly *her*. Not *things*."

I laid the vials in her hands and led her to Cherilynn's side. I backed away a few steps and sat down.

She knelt beside her daughter. Hesitantly, she picked up Cherilyn's hands, rubbing them gently. She took a deep, trembling breath. As I watched, she became the loving mother, and Cherilynn her baby child.

She put some oils on her hands and then patted Cherilynn's temples, the nape of her neck, and stroked her long, blonde hair. Then Cherilynn's mom curled up on the ground beside her daughter, grasping her hands, their faces close, murmuring soft words I couldn't hear. She might have been praying or telling a story or just talking. Perhaps she sang.

As I kept my vigil, Cherilyn's face gradually relaxed, her once-fisted fingers lying easy in her mother's hands. Filled with hope, I moved closer and laid my fingers on her wrist. Her heart's relentless thrumming slowed and evened. At last, she slept, drawing deep and peaceful breaths.

It wasn't exactly a miracle. Well, maybe it was. Maybe this whole journey was one big weird miracle.

CHAPTER TEN

Zack

I WHISPERED A PRAYER OF thanks that nothing worse had happened. I felt bad I hadn't been a better judge of character when Ferrell and Beak first arrived. I should have known better. I should have been more on my toes. I thought about when Ferrell first drew his gun, replaying it over in my mind. I thought of a hundred different things I might have done differently, including pulling my own gun and shooting the idiot myself.

Well, I probably shouldn't have done that.

But now we were rid of them, and Christian was alive and only a little more holey than he was before. There was no point in beating myself up about it now.

"Okay, let's look at where we are," I said. "Good riddance to those two, but we're still without supplies, and Christian isn't exactly 100 percent."

"I'm okay," Christian said, his breath wreathing his face in mist in the cold air. "And I've got some ideas for hunting. Lucky for us, we're traveling through some fairly unpopulated country. I'll bet the closer we get to Jackson County and all those people, the more likely the game is all hunted out. So it'd be good to get it while we can."

"You've done a bit of hunting before?" Trey asked.

Christian laughed. "You could say that. My family isn't your typical suburban household. Dad used to take us kids up into the Payson Lakes area for weeks at a time. We'd hunt and trap all our own food. Pretty country up there."

We decided to move as quickly as we could with Christian's injury—and I continually felt the need to press on. It never left me.

Our mission couldn't wait. But by the end of the next day, Christian didn't look so great. His face took on a gray cast, and although he didn't complain, he drooped a bit in the saddle.

"Let me take care of your horse," I said when we stopped to camp near Crystal Lake. He wordlessly slid from the saddle and handed over the reins. Trey started a fire, and Christian tossed his bedroll out and laid down, huddling beside the growing flame.

"I'm just tired," he said, but when Trey and I had a look at his leg, we saw the telltale streaks of an infection setting in. We dosed him with painkillers and smeared the wounds with antibiotic cream from our first-aid kit, but he was definitely not himself. It was like I was watching him fade.

We'd cleaned his wounds the best we could, but the bullet had traveled through filthy jeans into his leg. And then he'd fallen out of the saddle into mud.

This could be bad.

I thought about the time I'd been shot on our first trek. That had been bad too, but I'd been healed after receiving a blessing from President Green. *It'd be nice if he was here now*, I thought.

Then came a thought I didn't want to acknowledge. I'd been ordained an elder by Amélie's dad before I'd gone to Provo to join the Nauvoo Legion. I didn't really understand what that meant, but they'd explained to me that one of the privileges or duties of such a person was that they could perform blessings.

Me?

I remembered Lee explaining that blessings were commonplace among Mormons and that they didn't require a stake president, that her father—one of the rank and file in their ward—had blessed her many times. Still, the thought that I could or should bless someone seemed impossible. I thought about the priest in my Catholic church blessing the congregation. He wore special robes and held up a holy golden cross while he spoke, his voice echoing in the cavernous chamber. He didn't seem like a regular guy at all. I knew it was different with the Mormons, but I still felt awkward about blessing people. Good grief. I was nineteen years old. I didn't have a clue how.

Exactly how did President Green go about it? He'd laid his hands on my head, along with Dr. Wilson, but I couldn't remember much else. I'd been gut-shot, so I wasn't exactly thinking straight. There were some special words and then a prayer, but if there was a particular ritual to follow, I had no idea what it would be. I admit I sort of felt relieved. Maybe that got me off the hook. Then I felt ashamed for the thought. What if Christian got worse because of my reluctance?

An idea hit me. Trey. He was older than me, and I doubted he was a recent convert like me. He'd know what to do.

I pulled him aside. "I was thinking that maybe Christian needs a blessing. What do you think?"

I expected Trey to readily agree. Instead, he shrugged. "Maybe."

"Well, uh, can you do it? I'm super new at this sort of thing."

He put his hands up. "No way. Not me."

That baffled me. I gaped at him, speechless.

Trey folded his arms. "Don't freak out, but that's not my thing."

"Er. Oh." His unenthusiastic response confused me. If a person had the ability to do something that amazing, that beautiful, why wouldn't he want to?

The realization that such reasoning also applied to me made me squirm. Wasn't I doing the exact same thing? *But I would give Christian a blessing*, I told myself. *I really would, if I knew how.*

Another thought flowed into my head. A memory of my own blessing from President Green.

"Do you have faith that God can heal you?" he asks.

I hesitate. "Yes."

"That's all you need."

Trey interrupted my reverie. "I'm a member of the Church and all, but not like that."

Ah. Of course there would be different levels of Mormon-ness. I just hadn't encountered it before.

"That's all right," I said. *Do you have faith?* echoed in my mind. *That's all you need.*

I sent up a little prayer. *God, if you're trying to tell me something, please be very clear*, I prayed. I'm not great with the subtle approach. I searched inward. I didn't hear words, only the sensation of meaning.

The ritual, the oil, the words. They have their place. Remember, though, that God knows your heart. He knows what you need even before you do. But you must ask.

I looked at Trey, still standing with his arms folded. I looked at Christian, curled up on the ground, the fire casting flickers of light across his face. He clutched the blanket tight around his shoulders.

Okay.

I knelt next to Christian, my knees burrowing into the rough ground. I felt a little weird in front of Trey, but now, for some reason, I didn't care. I didn't put my hands on Christian's head though. It felt okay to keep my hands clasped in my lap.

"Our Father who art in heaven," I prayed, my words not much more than a whisper. "We need your help. Christian's leg is bad. We need to get the cargo to its destination, and we can't do that if he's sick. I know you can make him well if that's your will. Thy will be done on earth as it is in heaven. Amen."

I knew my prayer was sort of a garbled mix of my old and new way of praying, but I took comfort in the idea that God didn't mind. He knew my heart. Now it was up to Him.

Trey walked off to do something with the horses, his gait a study in forced casualness. I stayed where I was for a while, watching Christian. I felt good inside, but I still didn't know what was going to happen.

A few seconds ticked by as I watched. He didn't leap up from his blankets, instantly healed. Not that I expected that. He slitted his eyelids open and looked at me.

"Thanks, bro."

I nodded. "Need anything? Water?"

"Yeah, I could use some water, now that you mention it." He heaved himself onto one elbow.

"Stay put." I fetched his canteen and made sure it was full. I saw the first-aid kit lying there, and an idea struck me. Struck me hard. I pulled out the little packages of rolled gauze, scissors, tape, and whatnot until I found the bottle of pills I'd seen added to the kit before we left the cavalry unit, the bottle not found in a typical first-aid kit.

Amoxicillin. I tapped out three tablets.

"Take these." I handed the pills and the canteen to Christian. He tipped the metal container back, taking several long swallows.

What made me think of those pills at that moment? The thudding of my heart, overwhelmed by a hot flush of pure Spirit, was my answer.

Whew. It was going to take time to get used to this Mormon stuff.

"Look, I'm gonna lay my bedroll out right here, so I'll be close by. Let me know if you need anything or if you get feeling worse." I gathered my things, and when I returned, I noticed Christian had thrown back a couple layers of his bedroll, one leg sprawled out. He had fallen asleep, that fast. Perhaps it was a good sign. I tugged the blanket back over him and got myself situated nearby.

Soon Trey returned, and he rolled into his blankets with a brief "good night." He didn't seem angry or anything—just typical Trey—unruffled, unmoved.

In the morning when I awoke, my first thought was of Christian. He still slept easy, and relief shot through me. I walked down to the bank of the skinny little river we'd been following. The water was ridiculously cold, and although I knew I looked rough with my patchy young-blond-boy whiskers sticking out all over the place, I decided to forgo shaving. Maybe for the rest of the trip.

Trey joined me. "How's Christian?"

"He seems better."

"Good. Hope he can travel. We really have to get moving. We need to put some miles behind us." I shot him a sharp glance. I knew Trey was dedicated to seeing our mission through. Did that focus take precedence over concern for a friend? Should it?

As I had these thoughts, Trey went to Christian's side. While I watched from the river's edge, Trey checked and redressed Christian's wounds as tenderly as he might a child's and then helped Christian hobble away from the camp so he could do his necessaries.

I felt ashamed for doubting Trey's concern for Christian. Two good guys. I was lucky to have them on my team. Together we'd been through a lot already. The journey had many miles remaining, but it seemed I'd known them forever. I couldn't think of anyone I'd trust more with my life.

Christian insisted he could travel, and although his leg wasn't even close to healed, his color looked much better. "I can man up and sit on a horse. The poor beast is the one doing all the work, not me."

The jostling of riding horseback wasn't going to feel great on that leg, but I saw the hopeful, intense look on Trey's face. The mission needed doing. And I knew that if I was in Christian's place, I'd want to get going too. So we levered him into the saddle, and off we went.

I saw to it that he had the antibiotics handy so he could keep taking them throughout the day.

Was it a miracle? Or had Christian's body just responded to the benefits of modern medicine? I knew what I'd felt. And, hello, a team member had been shot through the thigh, and we hadn't lost a single day's travel time.

Christian was a rock. We rode all morning, and he kept a smile on his ruddy face. And then he really amazed me.

"There are deer there," he said, motioning to a patch of woods to our right. "We should get ourselves one."

"Huh?" I looked around, seeing nothing deerlike. "What makes you think so?"

He just smiled. But then he shared a few Porter family hunting secrets, and within an hour, Trey's shooting skills made it happen.

Christian showed us how to butcher the animal. Steam rose from the carcass as we cut the meat into manageable pieces. We gorged that night and set aside as much as we could carry. Luckily, we were living in a refrigerator (and sometimes a freezer), so we didn't worry about the meat spoiling. At least we wouldn't go hungry for a few days.

While we ate, Christian told us more amazing things he'd learned in Payson Lakes. He could fish as well as he hunted and knew which forest plants were the tastiest. I'd never met anyone as prepared to survive outside civilization as Christian. I already thought the world of the guy, and my respect skyrocketed even higher.

Which set me to thinking. Trey could shoot the lights out. Christian had survival skills. The choices behind our special team's members started making more sense—all except for me. Why had I been chosen? And not just as a member but as the leader, no less? I couldn't understand it. But I knew dumping on myself was pointless and would only make me an even worse specimen of a leader.

Others had faith in me, apparently. Those who selected me for the cavalry unit. Captain Christensen. The mysterious someones who'd organized this special mission with all its intricate plans. My teammates.

And then there was Lee. She'd said she loved me, so she must believe in me. She must have seen something good in me. I'd been blown away by that ever since she first told me she loved me as we sat by the temple reflecting pool in Salt Lake City.

And God. He'd thought me worth saving, both from my sins (the usuals plus killing a man) and from a bullet in my gut.

Now it was my turn to pull together some faith in myself.

+

Kansas. At last.

One day seemed like the next. Wake up shivering next to a dead fire. Force yourself to get out of your sleeping bag. Eat something, break camp, saddle up, ride. Stay close to water and grass but away from people. Ride some more. Always cold.

Twice we managed to barter for grain feed; another time we stole some. Not awesome, but Trey reminded us that our mission—if we could complete it—would save many people from starving.

We passed south of Topeka, circling Clinton Lake, closing in on our goal of the Independence area. For the entire trip, we'd been in rural settings, skirting towns and people whenever possible. But soon we'd need to ride through Kansas City.

I rubbed my cold fingers and unfolded the well-worn map with its sheet of handwritten instructions to reread the final paragraph:

Follow Kansas Highway 10 to Shawnee Mission Park. Traveling through Kansas City is dangerous, so we will send men there to meet you. They will bring you through to Independence. The men will check for you each day between Nov. 15 and Nov. 30.

At least we'd have help. I couldn't wait to let someone else be in charge.

On the afternoon of November 21, we rode into the park. Relieved that we arrived within the window specified, I scanned the park for signs of our escort. But we didn't see anyone, even after riding all around the sprawling acreage.

We settled down to wait. After all, they were to check in each day for our arrival, and that could easily mean evening. Or early morning.

We found a dead tree and broke off a few branches to start a fire. Christian hobbled the horses to graze nearby. I could hardly stifle the impatience I felt. It seemed the fire took forever to get going. I stamped my cold feet, rubbed my arms, and willed it to hurry, hurry. The men that were supposed to meet us—where were they? Hurry, hurry. I wanted this DONE. I wanted this little package safely out of my hands.

I wanted to be finished with living in the saddle. I wanted to be warm. I wanted to see Lee.

But the men didn't show up that night. We made our pathetic dinner, ate, and cleaned up. It looked like it was going to snow, so we pitched the tent and set up the horse shelter before getting into our smoke-stinky sleeping bags.

In the morning, we woke to a scattering of snow. I tried to quell my anxiousness as we did our small tasks. But the men didn't come. We saw no one whatsoever, the park grounds a smooth unbroken white.

Lunchtime. No one.

"Holy cow, Zack. Can you stop pacing?" Christian grumped.

"Sorry. I think I'll go for a run around the park," I said. "Just in case they're waiting for us in another part."

Jogging in my boots and puffy parka wasn't easy, but it was a way to pass the time. I passed an area marked "dog park" (seriously?) and another marked "disk golf course" (Frisbee?). Pretty sheltered growing up in Zillah, yes.

It took me an hour to make a circuit of the park, and I saw zero people. Not a soul. I came back into camp and flung my cold yet sweaty self beside the fire.

To sum up, we waited all day, and I drove my companions insane. After we'd been at the park forty-eight hours, we had a decision to make:

1. Keep waiting.

2. Back out, go around Kansas City, and approach Independence from the east.

3. Go straight through Kansas City like we would have with our escort.

It didn't make sense to wait longer. We were within the window they'd specified, and if they hadn't come after two days, they weren't coming at all. Something had happened to them.

Going around KC might be a good idea, but I didn't have enough information. My map didn't show how far the city actually extended. I had no way to know how far we'd have to circle outward to avoid it or whether coming from the east—or any other direction—would be any better.

Going straight through seemed to be the only choice but a terrifying one. The people who set up our trip had thought it was too dangerous without an escort, and I doubted they were exaggerating. Plus the fact our escort never arrived. Maybe they'd gotten hung up in the city.

But we absolutely needed to go through.

Our survival skills would be tested in a different way.

We sat our horses at the edge of the park, looking east toward the city. On the horizon, tall office buildings spiked upward. "Are you guys ready?" I asked.

They nodded. I led out.

We followed a river, which gave the illusion we were still in an unsettled place, since woods crowded the banks. We passed through a couple more parks and what used to be wildlife preserves, but the landscape looked more and more urban. Still, we didn't see many signs of people.

At last, in the late hours of afternoon, we found ourselves over-looking a sprawling neighborhood with houses, apartment buildings, boarded-up grocery stores, and strip malls sitting silently under the wintry sky. Glad for any kind of food, our horses cropped mostly-dead, grassy weeds while we paused. Everything looked deserted, dead. I could only guess at the danger the escort was supposed to help us through.

"I've got these silver coins Captain Christensen gave me. I was hoping we could use some of it to buy food now that we're in a city," I said. "But maybe there's no one around."

"I doubt this place is as deserted as it looks," Trey said. "There are hardly any people here compared to what there used to be, for sure, but we should plan on this area being controlled by gangs. And by gangs, I mean survivors who've banded together to control certain areas and acquire food. My guess is they'll try to keep us from crossing through."

"Food's gonna be super scarce by now," Christian put in. "I'd be surprised if we could find anyone willing to sell any."

I nodded in glum agreement. Our venison was nearly gone, and I was sick to death of it. *Get tough, Allman*, I told myself. We only have to hang on a few more days. The cold was making me cranky—day after day after day of being out in the elements wore on a guy.

I wondered how Lee and her family were doing with the cold. Their route was a ways north of ours.

There was nothing to do but to just plunge ahead. "Tell us what to do, Trey," I said.

"Follow me." Trey heeled his horse, and we rode down into the neighborhood, staying close to the buildings rather than the middle of the street. After a few blocks and still seeing no one, I was tempted to relax. Would we cross through without trouble? I noticed Trey rode with one hand curled around his handgun. Definitely not relaxed.

"Here it comes," Trey said. On cue, four guys stepped out to block our path. At first, I was surprised they'd attempt to stop us, with us being on horseback and them on foot. Then I saw their guns.

"This way! Hurry!" Trey's horse darted into a dark slot between houses. As Christian and I rounded the corner, shots ricocheted after us. We galloped through a couple of backyards, my heart thundering the entire time. People with real guns and real bullets were shooting at us. This wasn't the movies—where the good guys ride through rainstorms of bullets and never get hit.

Christian and I followed Trey's zigzag path through a network of side streets and parking lots, riding crouched over our saddles. Just when I thought we'd lost them, more shots rang out. This time, they came from the north, ahead of us.

"They've got some kind of communication," Trey said. "Old school walkie-talkies or something. I wonder how big their territory is. I'd say we're going to be massively outnumbered any minute. I'm thinking we ride hard, eastward, and try to cross their border. Be ready."

I touched my own handgun. Be ready, Trey said. Ready to shoot someone? To protect Christian and Trey, for sure. That I would do. And the little pouch in my pocket? Captain Christensen said many lives depended on it. It must get through. No matter what.

The sun sank against the horizon. Soon it would be dark. Maybe it would make moving through the city easier. Or harder. We were on unknown enemy territory—their turf. They'd know it well.

"Yah!" Trey snapped the reins, and his horse bolted forward, turning to the right. We followed, riding hard, on grass whenever possible to muffle the noise. When we passed over asphalt or sidewalk, the horses' clopping seemed frighteningly loud, echoing through the silence of the deserted city. It felt like we'd shined a spotlight on ourselves. Here we are. Right here. Come get us.

A few more shots flew past us and then stopped. We saw no more pursuit from the apparent gang, and we assumed we'd left their territory.

We entered Kansas City proper, which seemed endlessly vast. I heard the sound of gunfire, raising the hairs on my neck, but it apparently wasn't directed at us, sounding many blocks away. We kept the horses at a trot through tangles of streets, parking lots, and alleys.

So close. If nothing blocked our path, we were within a day or two of the Church compound. My heart raced with anticipation, thinking of that moment when I'd see the new city of the Saints and the temple under construction. And the moment when I'd successfully hand over the little packet and no longer have that pressure weighing on me. I wanted that moment so badly that I couldn't imagine trying to camp for the night within the city. I just wanted to press on. We didn't talk about it—we hardly spoke at all—but Christian and Trey seemed to feel the same.

Night fell. Stars pricked the velvet black of the sky, and I thought how only a few months ago the city would have buzzed with movement and light. Dark streetlights brooded overhead like metal vultures. The city seemed like a dead thing.

I remembered my trip to Seattle a couple of years ago. I'd been there only for the afternoon. My knowledge of cities at night consisted of movie and television images. I wondered if I'd ever see a big city at night the way it used to be—cars zooming, lights blinking, neon signs flashing punches of color. Maybe that chance would never come again.

We entered a narrow street running between rows of tall buildings. Halfway down, an even smaller alley cut between two buildings. "Let's pull up here," Trey said. "I want to watch a moment." As soon as we rode into the alley, I smelled a terrible stench. A dark shape huddled against the wall of the building on the right.

"Ugh, that's got to be a dead body," I said.

"Without a doubt," Christian agreed.

Trey sidled his horse so he could peer around the building at the street we'd just left. "Somewhere around twenty guys on horseback down there, coming this way," he said, his voice tight. "They're methodically checking all the alleys." He drew a deep breath. "Okay, look, this dead body gives me an idea. Zack, I doubt you're going to like it, but I think it's our best chance. Those guys coming—they aren't gang members like the others. I can tell they're military types. Chances are they've known our planned route all along. We're carrying something they want, and they won't stop till they get it. For us, the pouch is first priority. It has to get through. Period. So Christian and I are going to draw them off. You're going to wait until it's safe then go through."

"What?" I hissed. "I'm not going to let you do that. Too dangerous."

"We were supposed to be a decoy. So we'll be a decoy," Christian said. "For real this time."

Trey slid off his horse and walked over to the body. "We don't have time to argue about it. They'll be here any moment. Zack, help me." He hooked his hands under the body's arms and dragged it over by me. I repressed a shudder at its floppiness.

"This stinky piece of garbage is going to be you. We'll ride out of here with three guys on horseback. They'll never suspect we've swapped you out. You'll have to go the rest of the way on foot."

I spluttered. "I'm still not okay with you guys doing this."

"Hurry. There's no time. I know you're supposed to be the one making the decisions, but you've got to decide to do this. And now."

I dismounted. Trey bent over the body with his back toward the alley's opening. Looking over Big Black's broad shoulder, I saw a dark figure run into the alley. He held a gun pointed straight at Trey.

Everything slammed into super slow motion. I saw the scene play out. In one more second, the man would shoot Trey in the back. He would die.

My hand closed around the gun in my waistband. I pulled it out and leveled it at the man.

I shot him.

Blood surged, hot in my veins. The man crumpled, hit in the chest.

I realized Trey was shouting at me. "Zack! Zack! Come on!"

Shock spread over me. My feet walked to the body. My arms lifted. My hands tied quick, tight lashings. My head was dull and heavy, stuffed with cotton.

Trey and Christian galloped out of the alley, leading Big Black with his terrible load. They veered to the right onto the street at top speed. Behind them clattered twenty soldiers who never even looked into the alley where I huddled with a different dead body than the one that had lain there moments ago. Now I huddled with the man that I'd shot and killed myself.

+

I lay unmoving next to the dead man, although his closeness and the thought of what I'd done nearly made me throw up. I squeezed my eyes shut. I knew I'd agonize over my decision to shoot. But such moral gymnastics would have to wait.

The sound of my companions and their pursuers faded. I had to get moving, but shock deadened my limbs. I forced myself to roll to my feet.

The dead man lay facedown, dark blood pooling under his outspread arms. I felt duty-bound to turn him over and look him in the face—see the face of the man I'd killed. I nudged him over with the toe of my boot.

In the dim light, I couldn't see him well, but he looked about like I expected—a hard, cruel face with short cropped hair and bristling whiskers. *Give me a few years*, I thought, *and I'll look just like him.* That thought sobered me. Was I so different from him?

Except for the tattoo on his right temple. A star within a circle. What did it mean?

I wasn't sure what the significance of my little pouch was, but it wasn't hard to guess that the seeds must have to do with a Church plan for growing food. Was it the seed portion of the pouch someone was desperate to take? I guessed one of the main challenges for the Ogden government to become the dominant faction would be feeding people. Maybe they wanted this special seed to help accomplish that. But what if they wanted to take it from the Church so as to keep control of food supplies for themselves? To keep their thumb on people?

Or maybe it was the memory card they wanted. What information did it hold? How would it even be used, since computers didn't work anymore? Something tickled the back of my mind about special shielded containers that could protect electronics from the effect of an EMP. Yes, the Church was ultraprepared. They would have done this. Surely they had a working computer—or two or ten.

I knew the cavalry's cargo had included special equipment that the people at BYU had built. I guessed the card had some sort of schematics. Did the equipment have to do with getting electricity back on? I could easily imagine that the group that got power back and retained control of it would have a huge advantage over any other group.

Either way, I had a ticking bomb in my pocket. In my mind, a scenario played itself out. My team would flee as long and as far as they could, but eventually, twenty riders would overtake them. I prayed like I'd never prayed before that they wouldn't be killed, that they'd be taken captive instead. I hoped that their captors would consider Trey's and Christian's possible knowledge of the mission a reason to keep them alive. Alive long enough for me to rescue them.

Immediately they'd see that the third guy riding with them wasn't me at all but a dead body. The focus would be back on finding me at that point. They'd be looking for me in force.

I made myself admit that I'd have to evade them long enough to hand over the package before doing anything about Trey and Christian. It would be ridiculous to put the mission in jeopardy and possibly throw away their sacrifice. Mission first. Then my friends. And I'd have to be fast. I'd have to fly.

-+-

I ran through the dark streets like a ghost passing over graves, my steps as soft as I could make them. Twice I saw groups of armed men pass through an intersection, but whether they were gang or military, I had no idea. I heard gunfire all around me, but I doubted it had anything to do with my team. The city was engulfed in a war of its own.

My only chance was to pass unnoticed like a mouse—a very fleet mouse.

I jogged through dark streets lit only by starlight until my lungs and legs burned with fatigue. Then I walked, pushing myself as hard as I could. I missed Big Black, who'd faithfully carried me so many miles. I missed Trey and Christian more. I hated being alone.

I tried to remember that I wasn't alone. God was there. But it was hard, really hard.

The sun came up. I was completely spent. The running, the constant fear of being hunted down, the worry about the mission and my friends, the lack of food and water—all had drained me to a dry husk. When I passed a shop with a broken-out door, I ducked inside. After looking around and finding the place deserted, I couldn't resist curling up on the floor of a closet. I'd sleep for an hour or so.

I laid there, a ball of nerves wound up tight. Every muscle ached from being tense with worry and maintaining hyperawareness. Gunfire battered my ears. What was I thinking? I couldn't sleep. My team had bought me time, at high cost. I couldn't waste it. I rubbed my eyes and slapped my cheeks to drive away the grogginess.

My stomach felt like a hollow pit trying to pull itself inside out. I briefly looked through the shop, hoping for anything edible, but I only found broken glass and smashed shelves.

Oh well.

I pulled out the many-times refolded map Captain Christensen had given me, studying it until I had clear in my mind the way I'd need to go. I'd expected to be guided through this last part, but I'd do it alone. The last leg of my journey. Twenty miles. That's what I needed.

As I moved to the door to the street, I saw a bicycle leaning against the hallway wall.

Hey. Maybe.

I felt the tires. They were low but not flat. Rideable. I took it out to the sidewalk and jumped on. Soon I was hurtling down a decline, weaving around trash and debris of all kinds.

But hills go both ways, and while I found myself trying to pump the pedals up an incline, two guys stepped out from the shadows of a building.

"Hey! That's the guy in the drawing. The one the military's looking for," one shouted to the other. They started toward me.

I growled. Looked like the military had a reward out on me. What should I do? I hated to drop the bike and run. When the road leveled out, I'd regret it. Steering with one hand, I fumbled in my pocket till I found the silver coins Captain Christensen had given me. Would they stop for those?

I pulled out three coins and tossed them behind me, toward the guys. I heard the coins tinkle against the sidewalk. I kept pumping up the hill, hoping they'd at least stop to see what I'd thrown—and hoping the silver didn't just make me more tempting.

They did stop. I heard them exclaiming over the coins but didn't wait to see if they gave up on me for good. I crested the hill and whizzed down the other side.

By now the soldiers were surely back on my trail, our ruse discovered. But during the next few minutes, I only saw one guy, running furtively the opposite direction, wrapped in his own strange goals. The darkness would be on my side, I hoped.

The bike wasn't great, and the tires were getting worse. I nearly abandoned it a couple times but kept riding.

Suddenly, only a hundred yards in front of me, a huge blast exploded in the middle of the road, rocking me from the bike. I went down hard. My boots, so ideal for horseback, tangled in the bike pedals, twisting my ankle as I crashed. I sprawled on the sidewalk, stunned and groaning.

As I watched the street fill with combatants, I realized the crash probably saved my life. They had no idea I was even there. I hobbled to my feet, wincing when I put weight on my left foot. I righted the bike and climbed back on—a bit more dented, harder to pedal, but definitely easier than walking with a sprained ankle. Still, every round of the pedals shot pain up my leg.

According to the signs above the road, I had at last reached the suburb of Independence. Now I just had to get to the east side, where the map showed the Church complex. I pedaled through the darkness. As I passed, I noticed a few buildings with signs of candle or lantern light within, but the area was mostly swamped in black. Even the stars were obscured by clouds. I hoped I was riding in the right direction. Somewhere behind me, a woman screamed, one high shrill note. I gritted my teeth.

Ahead, my eyes fastened to a faint splotch of brightness. What could it be? I pedaled faster, drawn to it. There on a rise stood a large building made of some whitish stone gleaming dully in the cloudy moonlight. Spires on its top reached into the sky.

On the highest spire, I saw a glimmering light.

Maybe someone knew I needed guidance. Maybe the Spirit gave them a nudge. Or maybe that light was always there, shining the way for many people, not just me. In any case, it was perfectly clear that I was looking at a temple. I was in the right place. Happiness surged inside me. My mission was nearly complete. The pedals circled in a blur.

"There he is!" a deep voice yelled. Gunfire cracked the air, and this time it wasn't from a battle between Kansas City factions. Someone was definitely shooting at me. Bullets whipped by from behind.

My heart sank with fear and dread. This could not be happening! Not when I was so close!

Another shot brushed my hair. I fought with all I had to keep it together, to keep pedaling. My body tensed, waiting for the feel of a slug hitting my gut. I knew what that felt like. Well, I'd most likely be hit in the back rather than the gut. Not awesome.

The temple reared up in front of me, the light from the single lit spire sheening down its side. Now I saw that a white iron gate encircled it. The gate was shut.

"Hey!" I yelled. "Temple! Open your gate!" I didn't slacken my pace.

A shot blew through the spokes of my back tire. I rode on.

A man appeared at the gate, hesitating. My mind pulsed with terror. He had to open the gate now!

I shouted my name. "Zack Allman!" The man put his hand on the latch but seemed like he moved through a morass of syrup. "I'm Zack Allman!" Bullets zinged off the white iron. At first I thought the man at the gate had been hit. Then I saw him throw his weight against the gate. It swung open a few feet.

My lungs and legs felt as if they'd burst into flames, but I drove my feet against the pedals with desperate force, lurching through the opening. The bike slid across the gravelly path, spinning and skidding underneath the ground-shrouding branches of a pine tree just inside the gate, where I lay hidden from sight, insensible with fear and exhaustion.

CHAPTER ELEVEN

Amélie

It was November 1, three months to the day from when we'd left Utah. We were somewhere in Nebraska, and this was definitely not fun anymore.

It seemed I'd barely managed to fall asleep when a huge commotion outside our tent woke me up.

Someone shouted, "Men! Hurry to the medical wagons. Bring your firearms."

"Stay here," Dad instructed as he and the other men hurried outside, pulling on boots and coats. After a moment, Jarron followed.

Janny, who'd slept snuggled beside me, whimpered softly. I reached out and grasped her hand.

"It's okay," I said. "The men will take care of the problem, whatever it is."

Once again, I felt frustrated that in a group this size, something huge could be happening and we might hear nothing for ages. We might wait a long, long time in fear before we'd know what was going on. Would it be worse to hear nothing? Or to hear gunfire?

We waited. And waited. I thought I heard the crack of rifles firing, but it sounded far away, and I couldn't be sure. I did hear the drumbeat of horses galloping back and forth and the sound of men shouting to each other. I wanted to run outside and try to see if Dad, Jarron, or any of the other fathers from our group were okay, but I knew it would be pointless. I clung to Janny's hand, pushed my face into my pillow, and prayed.

Hours passed, or at least, so it seemed. Time was hard to gauge.

At last Dad returned—along with Jarron and the other men. My heart surged to see they looked unharmed.

Safe! Had it been a false alarm?

But right away I saw that something had happened. Something bad. The men looked super upset—Janny's father, Dave, in particular. His face was red and splotchy, a picture of rage and grief.

All of us who'd stayed behind chorused, "What happened? What's wrong?"

Janny's mom, Candace, leapt to her husband's side and gripped his arms. "Dave. What is it?"

"The medical wagons were raided," he choked out. "They took pretty much everything."

Candace's face blanked with shock then crumpled. "The insulin?"

He nodded. They both stepped toward Janny, but Dave hesitated, holding Candace back. "Don't scare her," he whispered. "We'll find more somehow."

The men explained—guards quietly ambushed, distractions created, and a raid that happened too fast to stop—but none of the "how" really mattered. What mattered was that the supply of insulin had been kept all together on a medical wagon in a special container to keep it cold, and now it was gone. Janny and the other diabetics in the group had no insulin, and there really wasn't any way to get more. Not in the world we lived in now.

Of course, many people besides diabetics would be affected by losing our medical supplies. But right now all I could think about was the little girl beside me, staring at her parents with wide eyes.

She knew.

Two days later, she was dead.

+

The light had gone out of the world. I trudged along behind the cart. Dad looked thin and tired, and I thought he might have aged ten years in the last month alone. In the evenings, after getting the tent group settled, he'd lever himself into a folding camp chair beside the fire and sit like a statue for the rest of the night. I ached for him.

Even though it didn't make sense, I felt responsible—that it was somehow my fault since I couldn't do my share pulling the handcart.

The truth was, even if I pulled that cart like a champ, it would have made very little difference to Dad's condition.

My pulling ability—a drop in the ocean. A grain of sand on our Mormon Trail.

Sadly, I could hardly remember the joyful feeling I'd had just a couple of weeks ago when I'd finished the project. All I felt was a dull gratefulness that I didn't have to work on it anymore. Where was that feeling of success? That I was strong and capable? I'd been another girl a universe away. I couldn't say why. I mean, I knew losing Janny was a deep wound. But I couldn't seem to shake loose of the gloom. What was the matter with me?

And then the snow began.

Of course, it had snowed before on our trip. But even though we'd complained about it, it hadn't changed things much. It hadn't built up on the roadway and had been mostly just an annoyance.

First came the soft flakes that melted as they sifted downward, but soon the snow began clinging to the grass and brush that grew alongside the road. From my place behind the handcart with Mom, I watched the snow settle in little piles on Dad's and my brothers' knitted caps and tired shoulders.

Whenever she pushed, Mom sang her sixties tunes in her thin, wavery voice. Sometimes she'd go through a whole catalog of hippie songs—"The House of the Rising Sun," "Blowin' in the Wind," "Crimson 'n Clover." Today she only managed "I Feel the Earth Move" before the effort to simply keep pushing took her breath away.

Back in Zillah, sometimes it'd felt like me and Mom's roles got twisted up. She'd never failed to provide home-cooked meals or sew me clothes—even attempted to make me a pair of jeans once—but when it came to being there for me . . . that was more hit-and-miss. She had her own demons. Sometimes I felt like I was mothering her. But then she'd resolve to do better and try to suddenly be a figure of strength in my life. If I didn't respond, she'd be so hurt. Most of the time I was just confused. I didn't know which Mom she'd be on any particular day.

Now it seemed our needs were stripped away to the most basic. All she wanted to do was help me keep going. And that's what I wanted to do for her too.

So cold. I was already wearing all the clothes I'd brought—two pairs of jeans, four shirts, a hoodie, and a coat. There was nothing else to put on, no way to get warmer. My cheeks stung, and my toes felt like frozen slabs inside my boots.

Before long, snow filled the sky, the air we breathed, the whole world, it seemed. I couldn't see more than a few yards ahead, and only the fact that I could still see bits of asphalt here and there told me we were still on the road. Luckily, we were so far back in the pack (horde?) that we didn't have to worry about that, only follow. The thousands of carts ahead of us scraped a path, but eventually snow began to pack onto the road in icy sheets. Jarron, who pulled alongside Dad, lost his footing on the slick frozen surface and fell, tumbling to the ground in a tangle of lanky limbs. Dad, in his semitrance of walk/pull, nearly rolled the cart right over him.

"I'm okay, I'm okay," he said. Mom and I both rushed to his side to help him up. I felt a lump in my throat as I brushed snow from his face with my mittened hands, his teen-boy face red and chapped from living in cold weather for months.

Impulsively, I hugged him tight and put my cheek against his. "Thank you," I murmured.

"Hey, Lee-lee." He hugged me back. "I'm okay."

"I know. Just thank you. Thanks for helping Dad. For helping us."

He released me and started back to his place, but Ethan had stepped inside the bar with Dad, already pulling. Jarron went to the back of the cart and pushed against it, boots scrabbling for grip on the icy, uneven surface.

I fell into step, my cane jabbing into the snow on the road. I turned my coat's collar up around my face and walked on, head bowed.

We heard a crack from just ahead, followed by the sound of objects crashing against each other. "Oh no," I heard a man cry. "The wheel's busted."

There in front of us, all across the road, lay the contents of a handcart. The cart itself lay on its side, one of its tall wheels in pieces. The family stood around it in helpless shock.

We all stopped and stared at the cart, the stuff, the family. I'd seen a cart break down before, but dealing with it had been a much easier matter. They'd simply dragged it to the side and made repairs. That seemed impossible now. The side of the road was nothing but a huge hump of snow. Plus, I couldn't imagine how to repair something when you couldn't even see what you were doing with all the snow in your face—even if spare parts were at hand. In no time, their belongings were first dusted with snow then covered, making little white hills on the roadway.

"What are we going to do?" the mom cried. The dad stood still, silently staring.

Dad set our cart down and stepped out from behind the bar. He looked at the wheel, picking up pieces and examining them. The man finally joined him, sorting through the mess.

Dad tossed a spoke to the side of the road. "There's no fixing this. There are spare wheels on the stake wagons, but who can say where any of those are right now?"

More carts came up from behind until six or seven had gathered.

"Well, come on," Dad said. He picked up some sacks of stuff off the ground and set them on top of our already way overloaded cart. The other men followed suit, cramming things into their carts until all the family's belongings were loaded and there was nothing left but the broken cart. They hauled it to the side of the road so it no longer blocked the path. Without another word Dad stepped behind our own cart's bar, lifted it, and threw himself against it to get it rolling across the newly accumulated snow.

The sight of that family's faces broke my heart. Now they didn't even have a cart—their stuff was spread around here and there on many different carts, and they looked lost as they trailed behind us. The dad pushed on the back of a cart that had taken some of their things, but I could tell he felt super awkward and out of place.

A few more steps and we couldn't see the broken cart anymore, with the curtains of snow in the air and the shroud of the stuff collecting on the cart. Like so many other things, we had to leave it behind.

Through the blizzarding snow, I saw Cherilynn bent over, hands on knees. I fought my way to her side and put my arms around her.

"Are you okay?"

She nodded. I looked at her face and saw tears frozen in rivulets on her cheeks. I remembered what she'd told me about being stressed, being scared. Was her heart wigging out? I couldn't imagine what it would be like to be dealing with this while dizzy and light-headed besides everything else.

"Your heart?"

"No, no. It's just hard. You know."

Yeah, I knew.

We struggled on, but when the wind picked up, blowing the snow sideways, up, down, every which way, the world became a swirling maelstrom of white. I couldn't believe what we were doing. I couldn't believe we were actually trying to move through this stuff. The wind increased.

Wind? Really? What. The. Heck.

Impossible.

Missouri never seemed farther away.

I hadn't fallen since the storm began, but every step made me ask the question: is this the one where I end up on my behind? I kept my non-cane hand gripping the side of the cart and hoped for the best. I waited and hoped for Dad to call a halt at any moment. Traveling (or attempting to) in this stuff was ridiculous. Shouldn't we be huddling in a tent right now? Yet he kept going. Was he listening for the leaders to give some official word? Were there even leaders still somewhere in front of us? It seemed like the world had shrunk down to the fifty-foot radius I walked in. Nothing else existed. I was barely aware of the other families struggling around us.

The freezing sting of snow slapped my face like a million little icy needles. I tried to hunker down deeper into my coat, but the wind slithered into the cracks and corners of my clothing, seeking out my skin. Howling filled my ears, stoppering them from any other sound.

My hand on the cart sensed that we'd stopped. Dad's form came through the snow toward me. He pulled me close, his arm a bulwark. Mom and the boys joined us, and we stood in a circle, the forehead part of our caps touching.

"Let's pray," Dad said. "Heavenly Father . . ." The wind snatched his words and tossed them away. I couldn't hear what he said, but I felt his plea for help. We added our own.

We said our amens. "Dad, shouldn't we get the tent up? Can't we put it up and wait out the storm?" I asked.

Dad's lips thinned into a line. "I have no idea where our tent wagon is right now," he said. "We have no choice but to keep going."

"But . . . But . . ." I stammered. "How will we ever find them?" We had to shout to be heard.

"Don't worry. We'll catch them when they stop. I know they're ahead of us somewhere. Hopefully they'll stop soon."

Mom started crying, and I bit my lip to keep from joining in. I'd never been this cold, this miserable.

I couldn't stop asking why.

God could stop this storm with a flick of a heavenly finger if He chose to. Why didn't He? I mean, here were two hundred thousand Mormons getting dumped on by a huge snowstorm. I bet a very large percentage of them were praying their hearts out. So why did it continue? It hadn't lessened one iota since we said amen.

Why?

Why not encase us in a bubble of sunshine? We were doing His will, were we not? Why was there no golden conveyor belt from Salt Lake City to Missouri?

Once I got on that crazy train, it just got worse.

We're going to die out here, I thought. *I won't see Missouri.* The goal I'd held in my mind of walking into a shining city on a hill—dotted with temples and happy people—now was clearly a delusion without a speck of reality to it. I wasn't getting anywhere near Missouri. I'd fall in some snow-filled Nebraskan ditch and freeze solid.

A new thought crowded in. *I won't see Zack either.* A choking sensation squeezed my throat like a steel clamp, and unwanted tears sprang free. *Maybe he'll look for me and never find me, not until next summer when this ridiculous place thaws. If ever. Or maybe he won't even look. Too much trouble. Perhaps he's already forgotten about me, with his super-important assignment and big adventures, rescuing Apostles and hanging out with the Three Nephites.*

Clearly, I wasn't thinking straight.

Maybe Zack wasn't the only one who'd forgotten me. As I gazed into the swirling whiteness obscuring the sky, I saw no miracle on its way. No angels holding dry wood, matches, and cups of hot chocolate. No blue sky shoving aside the clouds shedding sheets of snow.

I thought of the hundreds of prayers about my leg I'd sent upward over the years. There'd been no miracle there either. I rarely prayed about it anymore. For the most part, I'd accepted I was going to be this way forever and that God wanted it that way. I'd actually become okay with that, telling myself I'd understand why someday. But right now all the frustration and hurt came flooding back. *Why? Why? Why do I have to haul this broken excuse for a leg through knee-deep snow drifts for a million miles? Why? Why can't I have my miracle? God, you know my leg hurts right now. If you know everything, you know.*

Memories flashed through my mind—the Bluebird rolling within a whisker of my head, leaving it untouched before continuing over my leg instead; Zack opening his eyes and smiling at me, his terrible gunshot wound healed—I brushed them all aside. I must have been really cold because I was no longer sure they had happened.

I was no longer sure about anything.

—⎺|⎺—

At the moment it felt like hoping and praying for things was just too painful. Maybe it'd be better to close myself off. Freeze my heart. After all, it was half frozen already.

If I made myself hard and cold, it wouldn't hurt so much when my hopes didn't come true. It would be easier all the way around to stop hoping, stop caring. Then failing wouldn't matter. There'd be no need to try. And it wouldn't hurt so much when Zack dumped me because surely that was only a matter of time. Except that I'd probably die before he got the chance.

Instead of fighting the cold, I'd just embrace it. Let it seal me off from pain. Let it save me.

The snow billowing around me became more and more solid until I could feel it pressed against my face. Snow was everywhere, tight and hard and cold—in my nostrils, on my closed eyelids, rammed inside my ears. I could feel nothing else. I was enveloped in it. I was buried in it. I was a corpse.

I felt myself lifted. From a frozen stupor, I realized I'd fallen into a snowdrift. Dad's arms burrowed and raised me, cradling me against him. Snow fell away from my face, and I gasped for breath. Cold air sliced into my lungs.

He laid me down. But where was I? Underneath me I felt something lumpy—hard in some places, soft in others. Definitely not snow. Then some sort of fabric covered me—perhaps a blanket—shrouding my face from snowfall.

The ground tilted, and I felt a jerk forward. Then there was the sensation of motion.

I knew.

Dad had laid me on the handcart.

"No, Dad, no," I cried into the covering. My voice went nowhere. Strangely, although I was no longer bound up in snow, I couldn't move.

The cart didn't stop. All I could do was lie there and imagine what was going on outside of my blanket-cave. Dad would be pulling the cart with all his might through deep, drifting snow. One brother would be beside him. Another brother behind pushing. Mom pushing. An impossible load, now with my weight added.

On the first trek, I'd tried with everything I had to walk the whole way. To never ride on the green truck. It was so hard—the hardest thing I'd ever done to that point. For some reason, that goal had become very important to me. It kept me going. And when I achieved it, it filled me with a feeling of strength and accomplishment. When I realized we'd be going on another journey nearly twice as long and in the winter, I immediately decided I'd do the same. I'd walk every step myself. No cheating.

But not only was I not walking, my poor, cold, exhausted family was carrying me.

I cried until I could cry no more.

CHAPTER TWELVE

Zack

"Here's Brother Allman, sir." A clerk ushered me into a room in the sprawling administration building next to the temple.

Of course my arrival had created quite a stir. People had wanted to fuss over me, but I'd waved them all off. I only needed one thing—to see Ben Young. I wasn't about to wait one moment longer than necessary.

The office was sparsely furnished with a paper-strewn desk and two chairs. Behind the desk sat Ben Young, a man of maybe thirty years. The one I'd been told to find when I arrived. He wore a white dress shirt and tie; although the tie was pulled loose and he'd rolled the sleeves. He was balding, the remaining hair shaved close, and he wore a neatly trimmed goatee. A feeling of the Spirit poured off him. This was a godly man.

He rose. "How are you, son? Can I get you anything? Please, sit down."

I limped into a chair, noticing for the first time that I was completely filthy. My jeans were crusted with mud and blood (Mine? Christian's? The dead guy's?), my coat ripped and embedded with grease and gravel. I didn't want to think about what a mess my head was—dirty hair with three months' growth of a scraggily beard.

"This first." My hand shook a little as I dipped into my jacket pocket and pulled out the pouch, the one I'd carried so far. So much had been sacrificed to get it here. I set it on the desk and pushed it across.

"We want to express our gratitude to you, Zack. Words can't say enough to thank you for what you've done." Ben picked up the pouch, holding it like a sacred relic. "Give me one moment, if you would." He walked to the door and beckoned to the clerk who'd brought me in. "Please send for Brother Valentine. Have him bring a security detail." He returned to his seat. "We'll get this to the lab immediately."

"Am I permitted to know what I carried all this way?"

"Working prototypes for restoring the power grid were with the main calvary unit, but your memory card carries all the specs and information for recreating them. The prototypes would have allowed us to quickly get power back on, but we felt the card, being so small, had a better chance of getting through."

"And the grain?"

"The grain has a special enzyme that will allow it to grow and mature in half the normal time. Barrels of seed grain were prepared and loaded on the cavalry's wagons, ready to plant when they arrived. That was stolen too. But with this, we'll be able to recreate it. Information about the grain is also on the card, and we included some treated grain that scientists could reverse engineer in case the card was lost or unusable. The vial holds a sample of the enzyme."

I stared at the pouch in his hands. "So much effort for a little bag of seeds." The words spilled out of my mouth before I could catch them.

"Yes. But this little bag is going to save thousands of people from starving."

"Why did it have to be done this way? Why not let the government have this info? Wouldn't that let more people benefit from it?"

"We offered the Ogden government info on the enzyme, but they insisted on having control over who could make it or use it. It became clear they'd dole it out only in a way that would strengthen their position of power. Control the food, control the people. They wouldn't have permitted the Church to plant it in Missouri. As for the rest—the power restoration equipment—same story. Whichever faction gets power back first—with airplanes, helicopters, and so on—will quickly dominate the others. They'd essentially use our equipment as a weapon. So we tried very hard to keep that to ourselves. As far as we know, they haven't successfully deployed the stolen equipment yet. But it won't be long."

"Ben—Brother Young—can I just ask—why me? Why was I chosen for the three man team? Trey and Christian I get. But why me?"

"Why are any of us called to do what we do? You know how Church callings work, don't you?"

"Uh, no."

"The priesthood leader prays about it and receives direction, whether for a Sunday School teacher or a Beehive adviser . . . or a guy to ride horseback across the country. Many times our callings aren't what we'd expect, Zack. But we do what we can to help build the kingdom. When we're finished, we're released, and we prepare to receive a new calling."

"So someone—a leader—prayed about *me*?" I felt a shiver.

"Yes. And they knew you would be the one who'd be able to walk in this door, mission fulfilled."

I swallowed. "So is this calling completed, then? Am I discharged . . . er, I mean, released?"

"Yes, I suppose so. Are you in a hurry?"

"Actually, yes. I need to go back and find Trey and Christian. They put themselves in danger to allow me to get the pouch here safely. I owe it to them to go and help them. To tell you the truth, I'm pretty worried."

"Where are they?"

"I don't know, exactly. We were in downtown Kansas City when they pulled a stunt so I could get away. Last I saw, twenty men were chasing them. I assume they've been captured. I pray to God they're still alive."

Ben stood. "Let's see what we can do. There are people who want to talk to you about your trip, but maybe that can wait. You can't go alone, of course."

I thought about how long it would take to put together men for a team—to get horses ready, to make plans—and I felt I'd turn inside out for worry and anxiousness. I wanted to go now. But I also knew I had no idea how to find Trey and Christian. Going charging off blindly would do no good.

Besides, I didn't even have a horse. All I had was a piece-of-junk bike—which probably didn't work anymore after my dramatic slide into a pine tree—and a sprained ankle. Plus, my body felt like it was in even worse shape than that bike. I followed Ben into the hallway.

A voice floated toward me from down the hall, and although I couldn't understand the words, the voice sounded just like Trey.

No way.

I limp-jogged past Ben into a reception area. There stood Trey and Christian. I couldn't believe my eyes. I let out a whoop, and when they saw me, we fell into a massive three-man embrace, arms across each other's shoulders.

"You made it. Sweet," Trey said. "The pouch?"

"Safe and sound. How did you guys get away?" I asked.

"You shoulda seen us, bro." Christian grinned. "It was magical."

"Heh," Trey scoffed. "They chased us for a while, and it looked grim at first. But once they figured out you weren't with us, the love wasn't there anymore." He shrugged. "They let us go."

"No way. No way." I knew I was babbling, but I was so relieved I couldn't think straight.

Christian said, "Allman, you haven't had a real bath in weeks, and you stink. But I gotta say, the dead guy stank more."

I laughed. And laughed. Relief washed over me, making me sort of giddy. Finally it subsided enough I could speak like a human. I turned to see Ben standing nearby with a smile on his face. "It's so weird that we're here, that we're done. What do we do now?" I asked him.

"You've earned some rest," Ben replied, "and you clearly need it. But frankly, there's a situation we need your help with. Tomorrow we're sending out everyone we can spare to go back and help the main company. They're in trouble."

The main company! Fear lanced through me. Lee! Was she all right? "What's up?" I asked, trying to calm my voice.

"They've gotten into some severe weather. We're sending back supplies—fresh horses and oxen and wagons to bring in the ones who are worst off. What do you say? Can you be ready by tomorrow?"

"Absolutely." I looked at Trey and Christian. Their eyes burned with intensity. Both nodded.

"Count us in," Trey said.

We walked down the hall, the three of us in step—despite my ankle. "Hey," Trey said. "I just want to tell you guys it's been a real privilege being on this team with both of you. Zack—nicely done, man. Good job getting that pouch delivered. Not bad for your first command. And thanks for having my back when we were stuck in that alley. I know that wasn't easy for you."

My mind raced with memories of that split-second decision. I felt bile rise in my throat just at the thought. I coughed.

"Does it ever get easier?" I rasped.

"For some. I hope for your sake it never will."

—┼—

The people in charge of the rescue mission had the brilliant idea of assigning me, Trey, and Christian to ride out together. Plus, they reunited me with Big Black.

Sweet.

The Missouri leaders had put together quite a few wagons to take supplies out to the main company and to carry people back. They'd been working on this for a couple of days solid, and everything was finally ready. But because they wanted help to arrive as soon as possible—for morale reasons along with the practical—they allowed a few of us to take off while they finished the last preparations. The three of us joined nine other riders to lead out. The wagons would leave soon after.

We found out we'd gained a bit of notoriety as the "overland team." Christian basked in it, which made me laugh because he was one of the humblest guys I'd ever met. He didn't strut, but he loved the respect people showed us. He said it was kinda nice—and new—for a guy with five older brothers. He couldn't stop grinning.

That sense of belonging. He was feeling it, and that's what I drank in, as deep as I could.

"When we get to the main group, will your families be there waiting for you?" I asked Trey and Christian. Of course I thought about Lee and the Hatches, who were pretty much the only family I had now.

"Mine's not," Christian said. "My dad isn't the join-up kind of guy. They'll make it out here to Missouri eventually, I've no doubt. But they'll do it their own way. Besides, this first group is Wasatch Front people, and we're a bit farther south."

"Mine—well—I doubt it, but I don't know for sure," Trey said. "We haven't exactly been in contact."

"You and your folks aren't close?" I asked.

"No." Trey looked at the horizon, his face a stone. "I left home at fourteen, as soon as I could manage it."

Fourteen! I gulped. "That's rough, really rough," I said. I definitely hadn't been ready to be separated from my dad when he got killed, and I'd been eighteen.

"I wanted to be close to my dad," Trey continued, staring straight ahead. His voice was casual, but was that casualness forced? I couldn't tell. "I wanted so bad for him to be the dad of dreams. I'd ask him every day if we could play catch or go bowling or something, I wouldn't have cared what. He always put me off. I should have known he wasn't that kind of dad. In reality he was just a mean drunk."

Trey stopped speaking and swallowed, pressing his lips into a line. He took a deep breath, and I tried to send him some encouraging vibes.

He continued, his voice as matter-of-fact as ever. "When I was eleven, he finally agreed to take me fishing. I was out of my mind with joy. I got up early, got all ready, put together the gear, everything. He said he had to get something and he'd be right back. He took off in the car. I sat on the porch with my fishing stuff and waited. I waited for hours. All day. I kept telling myself, *He will come. He'll come. He promised.* This'll be the time when he finally comes through. When it was dark, he came back, drunk as usual. I was still waiting there on the porch. I followed him inside. I said, 'It's okay, Dad, we can go now. It's okay.' I was still so hopeful, ready to forgive. Then he grabbed me by the back of the neck and threw me down a flight of stairs. Broke my leg."

Christian and I stared from our places on either side of him. Trey's face remained emotionless.

"That's when I started planning to leave. As soon as I could, I went on my own. The minute I was old enough, I joined the army."

"What about your mom?" Christian said.

"She never stuck up for me when I was little, and by the time I got to be a teenager, I'd given up hope that she ever would."

"You said you were baptized," I said.

"Yeah, when I was a kid. But we weren't really church people. I was pretty surprised when the Church asked me to join this mission because I haven't been very active. I guess they needed my sniper skills."

Or maybe you needed this mission, I thought. *Even more than they needed you.* He sounded hurt underneath the grim-faced bravado.

"God will bless—"

He cut me off. "I know you mean well, but don't bother. It's true for you but not for me."

"What are you talking about?"

"You think I don't want the Church stuff? The blessings, the warm feelings you guys are always yammering about? I don't know why, but I don't get that. I don't get anything. I've heard a few million times that it's a small voice. I understand that. But for me, I guess it's not just small. It's microscopic."

I couldn't think of a single thing to say.

"It's okay, bro," Christian said. "That stuff will sort itself out. I know it's hard. Me and Zack, we're here for you. You can lean on us for anything—and that includes spiritual things."

Trey pressed his lips together and closed his eyes for a moment. I thought maybe he'd give some angry retort.

Instead he paused and looked at us each intently before brushing his hand over his eyes. Then he just said, "Thank you."

✝

Our conversation returned to regular topics like the weather, and things seemed pretty normal until we got close to the Nebraska border. The temperature hovered around freezing, and snow dusted the hills and roadsides. The road cut a black swath through the white expanse.

Once we crossed the border, the snow got crazy. I'd never seen snow like this, ever. In Zillah, we got a few inches each year, and it never stayed long enough to suit me when I was a kid. Now I saw knee-deep snow. Then hip-deep—incredible. Then snowdrifts as high as my shoulder—impossible. And it was still snowing.

We used the mile markers and road signs to approximate where the road was, but our horses had to break through drifts in many places. My boots kicked through it as we rode. I thought maybe our passage would make it a tiny bit easier for the wagons and teams that followed us. But the snow got deeper, and the wind blew harder, creating massive drifts. Wagons would surely struggle if they could roll at all. We took it slow, allowing our horses time to rest every few yards of breaking trail.

At last we met a scout from the main encampment. He told us the vanguard of the group was less than a mile farther. I could hardly believe it. A moving city of 200,000 people was right ahead, yet I could hear nothing. The snow muffled everything into a blanketed, heavy quiet.

And then there was the fact that the group wasn't actually moving right now. Snow clogged their way. They were stuck.

I couldn't stop thinking about Lee. She was close. So close.

"Hey, Zack, what's up?" Christian asked. "You look like you're severely caffeinated or something."

"Huh?" I looked down at my hands on the reins. They jittered and jumped, shivering like aspen leaves on a breezy day. No wonder Big Black seemed skittish with the way my knees were twitching.

I'd been trying to deny it to myself, but the fact was, I was almost overcome with anticipation—and nervousness—about seeing Lee. I'd see her *today*. Maybe even within the hour. My heart clenched.

It'd been over three months, and I'd had not a single word from or about her. So much could have happened. Lee had a heart like a lion, but I knew her. She might push herself beyond what was sensible, and there was no denying that the circumstances would challenge even the strongest man, let alone a petite young woman who, yes, I had to say it, had a less-than-100-percent leg.

On the first trek, I'd been there with her. I'd been able to help her, watch over her. This time I'd been far away. She had her family, but it rankled that I'd had to leave her. I needed to see with my own eyes that she was okay. I needed to make it okay.

What if she'd met another guy? After three months, it might easily have happened. She might have fallen for someone who had a better Mormon pedigree than me. That would be pretty much any guy on this trek.

What if the Hatch family hadn't even made it this far? Any number of things could have happened. I didn't even know for sure that they'd left with the main group, although I thought it very likely.

And then there was the unthinkable. She might have died. Such news couldn't have reached me. My hands shook so hard I clamped them over my saddle's horn.

I realized Christian still looked at me, a quizzical grin on his face. "You're going into boyfriend mode, aren't you, bro?"

"Shut up," I said, smiling to soften my words.

We came upon the encampment. Nothing could have prepared me for such a sight. Behind a massive snowdrift stretching hundreds of yards, tents speckled the white-covered roadway. It looked like the group had run up against the snowy roadblock and pitched camp on the spot. Tents, wagons, carts, animals, and people stretched out as far as I could see through the heavy snowfall, and I knew it continued for miles beyond my sight. It truly was a city of huge proportions.

We spoke to some leaders whose faces looked pretty tired—no, exhausted—from worry and overwork. When we told them wagons full of relief followed behind us, the brethren were overwhelmed. One guy started crying. Another sank to his knees right in front of us and thanked God.

"We want you to put us to work," I said. "But first, if it's all right, I'd like to see my—my family. I've got to know if they're okay."

"Absolutely," a leader said. He was probably an Apostle or something, and I felt dumb that I didn't know for sure. "The camps are arranged in stakes, somewhat alphabetically. Once you find the right stake, it won't be hard to find your family."

I felt my face sag. "Sir, I apologize. I have no idea what stake they are in. I've been off with the Legion—"

The man retrieved a folder from a box sitting inside a wagon nearby. He flipped it open. "What's the name?"

"Loren Hatch."

The man smiled. "Salt Lake Liberty Stake. Actually, I was about to send for a messenger to run out to them. I'll just let you deliver my message since you're going."

I nodded. "I'd be glad to."

"The message is actually for Amélie, the daughter. Your sister, I presume?"

"Er. Uh. Not exactly."

"But you know her?"

I glanced at Christian and Trey, whose eyes danced with amusement. Christian covered his grinning mouth.

"Yes, I know her." *I know her face better than I know my own*, I thought.

"Just tell Amélie that we need her help. If she could come up here and speak with us as soon as possible, it would be appreciated."

What was that about? I knew Lee had been asked to help out with the youth, but what did they want with her now, in the middle of this snow disaster?

Did the fact that he asked for her mean she was okay? How much current info about the thousands and thousands of individuals did the leaders know?

"Yes, sir. I'll tell her."

"You guys with me?" I asked Trey and Christian.

"Do you want us to be?" Christian asked.

"In my book, if there's a choice, we stick together." I smiled.

We rode down through the camp, reading the the stake banners as we passed. We often just called out to people to tell us which stake they were, since the banners were hard to read with all the snow. Farmington Utah North Stake. Heber City Utah East Stake. Lehi Utah Stake. When we got to the *S*'s, my heart started pumping hard.

Salt Lake Liberty Stake.

My eyes scanned the stake's camp—big tents with central poles scattered across the trampled snow, handcarts clustered around them, people moving about—hundreds and hundreds. I didn't see anyone I recognized. We wove our horses down through the group.

"You looking for someone, son?" an older man asked.

"Yes—Loren Hatch. Do you know where his camp is?"

"Probably back there." He pointed farther down.

Then I saw the familiar head of scattered, thinning dark hair. Lee's dad bent over a cookfire. And there was Jarron—and Ethan too. My heart leaped in my throat.

"There!" I pointed. We rode closer. But where was Lee? I forced myself to breathe.

We stopped just outside their campsite. I slid from the saddle and handed the reins to Trey.

I walked up, and all three Hatches turned. Their faces lit up, and I broke into a cheesy grin.

"Hey!" I said, reaching out my right hand.

"Zack! Is that really you?" Loren grasped my hand and then pulled me into a hug. We slapped each other's backs. Then I hugged Jarron and Ethan.

"What's up? How did you get here? We heard your cavalry unit had your own mission."

"Completed," I said. "Meet my companions—Trey and Christian." I motioned toward where they still sat astride their horses. They lifted a hand of greeting and nodded.

"Hello. Thanks for keeping Zack safe and sound," Loren said.

He must have seen my eyes darting around the campsite. "You must be anxious to see Lee-lee. She's in the tent sleeping."

That seemed odd in the middle of the day. "She's sleeping? Is she okay?"

"Yes, she's doing all right. She doesn't sleep so good some nights. Go ahead. She won't mind you waking her."

Ethan laughed. "She won't mind, believe me."

I walked toward the tent, my heart making a racket in my throat. Ducking through the tent flap, I took in the interior. Bedrolls were stacked against the sides, and other than a few miscellaneous bits of clothing here and there, the tent looked pretty empty. No people.

Except for one.

I tiptoed toward the far side where a little lump of blankets huddled. I couldn't see Lee's face—she had a stocking cap pulled low over her head, and she was burrowed deep into the blankets. But I'd recognize the brown waves of hair that spread across her pillow anywhere.

She was okay.

I knelt beside her and softly laid a hand on her shoulder, praying I wouldn't scare her. "Lee?" I whispered.

She sighed and turned toward me, still asleep. I gazed at the face I'd yearned to see for so long. With her dark hair, fair skin, and rosy cheeks, she could have been a modern Snow White. Then I saw that the rosiness was from living outside in cold weather—her delicate skin chapped. My throat tightened at the sight. She'd been suffering, I could tell. I couldn't stand it. I hadn't been there. I knew it wasn't my fault. I'd had a duty I had to fulfill. But still, it hurt inside. More than anything.

CHAPTER THIRTEEN

Amélie

AFTER DAD HAD PUT ME on the cart, I'd lain under my shroud for an hour, maybe two, the cart lurching beneath me. I heard only vague sounds filtering through the blanket.

The cart stopped. Often as we traveled, there would be temporary stops and starts to readjust the load or the pullers. But after a few minutes, I still noticed no motion. *Dad was probably too tired to pull me any farther*, I thought.

I felt frozen stiff, but I reached up and pulled away the covering—actually several layers of blankets. Instantly, my sight was filled with blinding light and snow.

"Lee." I felt Dad's hand on my head. "Lee, darling, are you all right?"

"Dad!" I couldn't explain or repress the emotion that came spilling out. Somehow, I was angry and grateful and resentful and adoring all at the same time. Tears choked me. I couldn't speak anymore.

"Hey, hey, don't cry." Dad leaned over the cart, bringing his face close.

"You—you know I didn't want to be carried," I finally managed to say. It didn't make sense, but I felt betrayed. He'd left us on our first trek, and we'd struggled all that way alone. Now he'd put me in the cart, taking away the chance to meet the challenge to carry my own weight. I knew it was crazy to feel betrayed. With the first trek, he'd only left because he absolutely had to—the Church needed him—and he knew we'd be fine. And we were. And now—he was only trying to help me. I knew this.

"Lee-lee, I'm so sorry. I'm so sorry for everything. I wish things were different. I wish I hadn't been gone when the attack came. I wish so much that I could have been with you on the first trek. And I wish—I wish, when you were little—I wish I'd checked more carefully when I pulled the pickup out that day I ran over your leg."

Dad's face looked miserable. Oh my gosh! He blamed himself for that? That was not even remotely his fault.

Dad continued, "And I wish you didn't have to be cold and sad and hurting."

I threw my arms around his neck. "Oh, Dad, I love you. I'm sorry I'm such a burden."

"Now, Lee, you must never think of yourself that way. You don't know how you help us. Maybe you can't pull the handcart. Maybe right now you can't even walk. But you are helping us all the same." He smiled, his weathered face creased with lines. Then he drew a deep breath and sighed. "Besides, it sort of doesn't matter about the walking at the moment. The group's halted."

"Now? Why?"

"They say that ahead, a monster drift blocks our road. I'm afraid we're going nowhere till this storm ends and we can dig out."

That night, like so many other nights, I only slept fitfully. I never could get warm anymore and sleep was elusive. After lunch, I crawled back into my frigid little nest of blankets for a nap. Why not? I was pretty much useless, and the group was stuck anyway. Might as well.

But as usual, the nap idea didn't go too well either. I swam in and out of sleep and had just gone under again when I felt something tugging me back to wakefulness.

". . . Lee . . ."

I cracked my eyes open, and there, hovering over me, was Zack.

But of course, it couldn't really be him. It was a dream Zack. I dreamed of him all the time. But for once this dream didn't seem to be about him getting riddled with bullets or some other nightmare. I held very still, willing the dream to continue.

"Lee."

I sighed and turned over, still half enfolded in sleep. I felt a light touch on my face, brushing back a tendril of hair.

I opened my eyes. Zack. Eyes full of concern and emotion, shaggy, brownish-blond strands falling across them. I supposed I was still dreaming, but then I felt my body—my real, awake body—being lifted from my pillow. I felt Zack's familiar arms close around me, and I knew. Somehow, incredibly, impossibly, Zack was really there.

I grabbed him tight, my fingers clutching handfuls of his parka, too scared to ever let go for fear he'd disappear. An hour ago when I'd laid down for a nap, I didn't know how I'd ever make myself get up again. So tired. So discouraged. My stupid, useless leg hurt worse than it ever had. Bitter. Angry.

"Zack! How can you be here?" I pulled away just enough to see his face. His face—the face I'd grown up with, watching him smile, laugh, scowl, smirk, grin, and, twice, cry: the day his father was killed and then the day he was baptized.

He looked changed, beyond the length of his hair and the extra ruddy brownness from living outside. What had those eyes seen? He wasn't crying at the moment but almost.

"Lee, I've been so worried," he said. "I'm here on assignment, but I had to come and see you first—before I get sucked into something."

"Don't say you're leaving again!"

"No one knows for sure."

I didn't want to consider that. I remembered thinking only a day ago that Zack didn't really love me. That it was only a matter of time before he saw how weak and broken I was, and then he'd be gone for good. But now, beyond all my hopes, he was here. What did it mean? I felt happy, confused, surprised, and scared all at the same time. He'd found me, huddling in the tent. Not helping. Not walking.

He'd seen.

Shame lanced through me. Tears leaked from the corners of my eyes.

"Lee, what's wrong?"

I gulped, trying to speak. "It's been hard, Zack. So super hard." Days—no, weeks—of cold misery swam up in my mind. "We haven't even gotten out of Nebraska yet, and two days ago they put me in the cart, Zack. *They put me in the handcart.*"

A look of pure anguish crossed Zack's face. At first I thought he felt ashamed for me, but then I knew. He knew, in a way only Zack could, how that fact hurt me. How it crushed me. He felt my pain. He hurt because I hurt.

Because he loved me.

He put his hands on my face, and his thumbs stroked my cheeks. Then he kissed me.

Oh. Oh.

His fingers swept the tears from my cheeks, and for the first time in three months, I felt truly safe and warm. How I adored those hands, those rough, calloused hands.

"Lee, it kills me to see you suffering. I know it's been hard, really hard. But you're strong. I know you can make it. And remember, you and God—you're just like this." He held up two crossed fingers. "I know He will help you. You've got to trust Him."

I gazed into his eyes—usually peaceful blue, now intense. The new Zack. I'd known he'd become a believer, but I hadn't seen this confidence, this conviction.

While he'd been away, he'd gotten solid.

He'd called me strong. I used to think of myself that way—could I be again?

If he believed I could do it, maybe I could try one more time.

"Where have you been, Zack? Is it still a secret?"

"I'll tell you all about it, I promise. Soon."

"You're here on assignment? Haven't you done enough? Can't you stay with us now?"

"I'm still on active duty. I have no idea what they've got in mind for us next. But there's at least a chance I'll be helping out here with the main encampment. I'll hope for that. And you aren't done yet either. The leaders at the front asked you to come up. There's something they'd like your help with."

"Me?"

"Yes, you."

I sighed, trying to hide a cringe.

"What's wrong? You don't want to?" Zack's forehead lined with worry.

"No, it's fine. It's just that—well—my leg has been bothering me a little, and it's a long way to the front."

"For you to say it's bothering you a little means it hurts bad." Zack frowned. "But don't worry about getting there. I'll take you on my horse, Big Black." He pointed a finger in my face. "No silly arguments about having to walk on your own."

"Yeah, no trouble there. I gave up on that already." It hurt how readily the old bitterness rose up within me. I thrust the feeling away. Zack was here! I could be strong. And riding horseback with him wasn't terrible either.

We ducked out of the tent to see Dad and the boys grinning at me. I grinned back. Two guys I'd never seen before stood beside their horses and held a third, a monstrous black beauty.

They grinned at me too. Everyone grinning.

"Where's Mom?" I asked.

"Off helping with a new baby," Dad said. "How are you doing?"

"Great now." More grinning.

Zack beamed at the two strangers and then turned to me. "Lee, I've been so looking forward to this. Meet my companions." He pointed at the solidly built young man with dark hair on the left and then the ruddy red-haired one wearing a cowboy hat. "This is Trey, and that's Christian. We've spent the last three months together—"

"I know, having adventures."

"Guys, this is Lee. My girl." Zack looked proud to say that, and it made my insides flip-flop to hear it.

Christian tipped his hat to me. Trey nodded.

Was I dreaming? Even though my hand was around Zack's arm, I still couldn't believe he was here.

Zack turned to Dad. "Sir, the leaders asked if I'd escort Lee up front. They want to speak to her."

"What about? Her young-people project? That's been done for some time now."

"They didn't say. If it's okay with you, I'll take her on Big Black with me."

Dad nodded. "I know you'll take care of her."

"I promise." Zack led me to the side of the giant black horse and boosted me up into his saddle. Gathering the reins, he swung up behind me. Snow still blew and swirled around us.

"Ethan, could you fetch my notebook?" I asked. I'd already turned in all the information to the leaders, but maybe I'd need my notebook for some reason. Better to be safe. Ethan dashed to our handcart, grabbed the notebook from my backpack, and handed it up to me. I slid it inside my coat.

Zack directed the horse carefully between the tents and people with Trey and Christian following behind. I realized that Zack was the leader of this little team. That stunned me and made me proud at the same time.

I'd never been to the front of the encampment, but when we got there, I saw it was pretty much the same as the rest. Tents, wagons, and handcarts, and in front of that, a wall of snow that seemed to have no end.

We dismounted. "It's real nice to meet you at last," Christian said.

"Yeah. We finally see who Zack's been mooning over the last three months," Trey added.

Flip-flop. "I can't wait to hear all about your trip," I said.

An elderly man approached us, sloshing through the trampled snow.

Zack tucked my arm under his—I'd forgotten my cane. "Hello again," he said. "Here's Amélie Hatch for you."

"Thank you. Hello, Sister. I'm Elder Wright." We shook hands. "We're hoping you can help us with an idea we have for getting out of this mess." He waved a hand toward the snowy barrier.

"Uh—sure."

"We'd like to utilize the young people to get us through this monster drift. On the list you created, there are thousands. We want to gather them all here at the front, where their sheer numbers and young energy can break us a trail. How do you suggest we gather and organize them?"

I gulped. He was asking me? I thought quickly.

"You have a system for contacting the stakes, right?" I asked.

"Yes—we send riders."

"I've got contact people among the youth in each stake. Maybe you could send messengers to the stakes with the youth leaders' names. Then they in turn gather everyone and tell them to head to the front."

"Hmm. Yes. Excellent. You have a list of these youth leaders?"

"Right here." I pulled out my notebook.

"I'd like you to prepare the names to hand to our messengers. And take charge once your youth arrive."

Take charge. Of thousands. He must have seen my face flood with panic because he smiled and grasped my arm. "Sister, you'll be great. We'll be here too."

"All right. Give me a few minutes, and I'll have the names ready." I limped over to a wagon and hopped up to sit on its edge. I flipped my notebook open and tore out a few blank sheets from the back. Then I opened to the front, to the first stake, Alpine Utah Stake. The young people who'd helped me gather names had little stars beside their names. I copied them, along with the stake name, on a blank sheet. As I wrote, snow covered the sheet. I blew across it every few seconds to clear it.

"You guys want to help?" I waved papers at Zack, Trey, and Christian. They bummed pencils off one of the leaders, and we started scribbling. When we had full sheets, we tore the papers into slips that could be handed to each stake.

When we finished, messengers took the slips out on their routes throughout the encampment. All I had to do now was wait. And get so, so nervous.

Snow still came down in frozen sheets, blown and tossed by wind. The barrier in front of us looked ridiculously high. Impassable. But as the youth gathered, the snow and wind both tapered off.

We were ready for our miracle.

—†—

Hours later, I watched as thousands of young people marched into the drifts. Break us a trail, I told them. They threw themselves into it, launching themselves across it, using their bodies to flatten and pack it down. They yelled like wild things, trampling out their frustrations about being stuck here, being cold, being exhausted. The barrier slowly fell beneath them. They laughed and pressed on.

I wished I could have been part of the human snow-trampling machine. It looked fun—and cathartic. Even Cherilynn got to help. But once I got things started, I contented myself to watch on the sidelines, as usual. Somehow, standing there clinging to Zack's arm didn't seem so bad. Not bad at all.

The youth went at it for the remainder of the day, and when the new day dawned, they rose and attacked the snowbank again. Finally, in late afternoon, we heard whoops come from far down the snow road being built, and moments later, young people came rushing back.

"Wagons! Lots of them! Loaded with supplies and food—and empty ones, too, to carry people."

Zack smiled. "They made it. It's about time."

+

News of wagons from Missouri spread through the camp in a snap, it seemed. People surged forward, filled with new hope. The youth who'd worked so hard breaking a trail through the monster drifts now carried people forward to the wagons—on their backs or cradled in their arms. Young men carrying little old ladies, some still in their sleeping bags. Pairs of girls bracketing others, young and old, arms across shoulders.

I cried when I saw it.

Others jumped in to help push and pull handcarts. Some of the young people who'd been the loudest of the complainers were now caught up in this feeling.

No one carried me to the wagons. I wasn't about to be carted off somewhere, not while Zack was still here.

Well, he was kind of still here. He, along with Trey and Christian, had been reinserted into the regular Nauvoo Legion, doing patrol duties along our flanks. The reality was that we still had a ways to go. That was hard, but I did get to see Zack most evenings. It kept me going.

When we got to Jackson County, there wasn't a big moment of arrival. It was more like we gradually got there. On the day we crossed the Missouri line, I thought about how I'd felt when we finally got to Salt Lake City. I'd been so overwhelmed by emotion at actually making it that I hardly saw the city. Then seeing Dad for the first time—to see that he was safe and alive—pretty much dissolved me.

I waited for that "hurray" feeling as we entered Jackson County. Yes, I was happy I'd made it, even though I hadn't walked the whole way, even though it was so stinking far and hard. But I was too tired to do a happy dance. And I couldn't dance anyway with my ridiculous leg. All I could really say was okay, now we're really at the end. I'm not going on any more journeys. This is it. I'm gonna wait right here for the end of the world.

We left the freeway and started down a much smaller road winding between harvested fields and pastures. There was only a light dusting of snow—so different from what we'd struggled through in Nebraska. It almost seemed odd to see bare ground after so much snow for so long.

Since I was way back in the huge pack, I didn't hear any announcement or anything about why we turned this way. We all trooped along obediently, bunching together on the narrower road.

I looked at the stubble-covered acres with curiosity as we passed. How had they cut this wheat? Threshed this corn? Had they gone out there with scythes? Then we came to a field that really opened my eyes. Men with teams of oxen plowed the earth. As we passed, I tried to see what sort of machinery they used. The plows didn't look super old nor brand-new either, though it was hard to tell for sure from where I walked. I guessed they'd taken regular plows, like tractors used to pull, and rigged them to be pulled by animals. Slowly, methodically, they worked their way across the field, churning the earth and stubble.

"Getting ready for planting winter wheat, looks like." Dad said. "Pretty late though. Maybe they can get away with it this far south."

Wheat. *Good*, I thought. *We'll need it.*

On we walked. After an hour or so on this smaller road, I heard a buzz of excited chatter arise from the people in front of us. Hands pointed ahead.

In the distance a cluster of large buildings appeared on the skyline. We asked each other what it was, but no one around us knew. The road seemed to point straight to it. I smiled. I hoped whoever waited in those buildings was ready for an onslaught of hungry, tired Mormons.

I had plenty of time to study the buildings while we slowly approached. The closer we got, the more amazed I became. There were tall buildings—though not skyscrapers by any means—medium-sized ones, shorter ones, and a whole cluster of silos and storage buildings. But nothing prepared me for what I saw when we came to a halt.

A city. A whole city, in a grid of neatly crossing streets. Right in the middle of all that farmland. Squat, modest houses interspersed with apartment buildings. A huge park. Churches. Shops, although I couldn't tell what they sold. A school of some kind. All new. This was only what was within my sight; the grid stretched beyond my vision. It looked like the pattern repeated itself across the grid, clusters forming little townships within the city.

Evidence of even more construction was everywhere. Workers swarmed the unpaved streets with oxen-drawn carts full of materials. I saw lots of women working, as well as men and young people too. Everyone seemed to be in a hurry.

I guessed they were building the city for us and the many more who'd follow. No doubt we'd have a lot to help with once we got settled.

Men on horseback rode along our flanks. They stopped momentarily here and there to shout directions, telling us to gather in our stakes and sit down together in the park where we'd be given further instructions.

We found our gathering place. An hour or so went by. Dad, Mom, me, and the boys enjoyed kicking back, cooling our heels. We'd done precious little of that over the last few months. At least it wasn't freezing cold. It was about forty-five degrees—funny how that seemed like short sleeve weather after where we'd been. I waved at Cherilynn, whose family sat near us. She seemed to have weathered the last bit of the trek, although she looked pretty bedraggled. Didn't we all?

The stake president stepped up and out came a megaphone.

"I have here a list of assignments," President Carroll said. "When I call your name, please come up as a family. I'll tell you where you'll be living. As you can see, the city is under construction, but there are places for everyone here. Many more people are coming so a lot of the work assignments have to do with building or supporting the building projects in several ways. Please be gracious about your housing assignment. Generous people have built these homes for you, and although you may have lived in something grander back in Utah, please appreciate what they've done for you. Most of the homes are exactly the same, so there's no need to wonder if you're being slighted somehow. The homes are modest, but they're livable. After months of camping, a roof over our heads is all we need, right? Some people are assigned to the apartment buildings. This is of necessity.

"When you go inside your home for the first time, you'll notice they are plain and quite empty. Workers have raced to complete enough homes for all of us, and they have done a miraculous job. This has been in preparation for years. But there hasn't been time to provide furniture. This will be part of our work to come. Please be patient and do all you can to help, and this huge undertaking will be successful.

"You'll be given some initial credits to purchase food and other necessities for your family at the bishops' storehouses located throughout the city. Thereafter, you'll earn credits through your work assignments. Everyone, no matter what their ability is, will have a chance to serve and earn credits. There is a place and a job for everyone, even if their circumstances allow them to do nothing but pray."

I stared in amazement at the rows of houses across the street from the park. The amount of time, money, and sheer hard work put in to building them staggered me. Surely they'd been working on it long before the power went off. Before Dad arrived on his super secret mission.

I felt a yearning inside start to grow to somehow be a part of this great building effort. I couldn't climb ladders or nail shingles on roofs, but hopefully there'd be something I could do. Something that would make a difference. I had the thought that "my" young people, every bit as much an army as the Nauvoo Legion, had a giant potential to get stuff done. Important stuff.

My wandering attention came back to President Carroll. "You might be worried about finding your house," he said. "But when you see your address, you'll be okay. You're all from Utah, so the grid system for street names will be familiar. The Church has been buying other properties in the area, especially around the temple lot, but those homes are already occupied."

Heads nodded; then someone called out. "Is the temple completed?"

"There are numerous temples under construction."

A prophecy I'd learned in seminary tickled the back of my mind about the temples that would be built in Jackson County. A shiver ran down my spine, the same one I got every time I thought about how these old prophecies were coming to pass right before my eyes. What else would I see? Many of the prophecies didn't sound fun at all. I gazed at the untroubled scene—people listening attentively, the pristine new houses and streets gleaming in the December sunshine. I knew war was coming. Armageddon? Yes, someday, somewhere. Would soldiers march down these very streets? What would happen to the peace of this place?

And the weather—what about that? Plagues of insects? Disease? There were more—terrible, terrible things I didn't even want to think of.

People always said that the righteous need not fear, but that didn't necessarily mean they wouldn't have trials or troubles. I knew plenty of righteous people who had serious problems. This very group had endured huge trials during our journey.

Could I trust that this place would protect me?

"How many people are going to live here total?" another person asked.

"I don't know. It's going to be big though. Really big."

"What's it called? Has it been named?"

"Oh yes, it's been named." President Carroll smiled. "Welcome to New Jerusalem."

CHAPTER FOURTEEN

Amélie

WHEN WE GOT TO OUR little house, it looked just like President Carroll described. Small, plain, and sturdy. Like the other houses on the street, it sat in a tidy square on a small patch of bare earth. A window looked out on each side of the front door. The outside was still unpainted. We rolled our handcart right up to the step in front of the door.

Dad turned the doorknob. Unlocked. He pushed the door open, and the five of us crowded inside, excited to see the place we'd now call home.

The door opened directly into a room that ran across the entire front of the house. A fireplace sat on the left end, with a black iron stove set into it. There was nothing else in the room—nothing at all. I mean, we'd known the house would be empty. President Carroll told us that. But it still hit me strangely somehow. Even the floor was bare planking.

In the middle of the room was an opening to a hallway. We found three tiny bedrooms and a bathroom opening off it. I looked at it a bit longingly. President Carroll had said the houses were built with plumbing stubbed in, but right now there was no running water. The bathroom had nothing but various pipes sticking a few inches out of the floor and wall.

It'd been a long time since I'd had an official bath, and it looked like it would be quite a while yet.

At the end of the hall, a door led out the back. Several yards away was a no-nonsense outhouse. I sighed.

At least we were here. No more walking.

I stepped into what would be my bedroom and put down my backpack. An uncontrollable giggle burst out. Some bedroom. Just a ten foot square, without even a bed in it. Apparently, until some future date, I'd sleep on the floor. I shrugged. Funny how little that mattered anymore. Actually, a nice flat floor with no roots poking my back didn't sound bad at all.

The room did have a door. There'd been precious little privacy in my life since we left Zillah last spring. So that would definitely be nice.

"Next task: the bishops' storehouse," Dad said. We trooped back outside and followed a stream of people down the street. Each ten block area had its own church building with a bishop's storehouse attached. Both were plain, without yards or even paint. That would come, I supposed. I liked the plainness. This was no time for frills.

The storehouse had a long counter, behind which were floor-to-ceiling shelves. Large barrels sat on the floor. It had the look of an old general store. But the shelves and barrels were empty, at least for now. We joined a line of people who were exchanging one of their credits for a prepacked sack of supplies from a huge pile in the corner of the room. Workers also handed a tin bucket for water to each family. A sign on the wall stated that a small supply of firewood had been delivered to each house's backyard already but that, in the future, we'd purchase it here at the storehouse.

It took all of a minute. Everything was super organized—it felt like we rode a wave of people into the storehouse and back out again. We hardly had a moment to nod to our new neighbors, and we were on our way back to our house.

Once we were on our own block again, we noticed an old-timey-looking water pump on the corner. We'd walked right by before without noticing it. Now there was a line of people with their shiny new tin buckets. The guy at the head of the line worked the handle up and down while water gushed into his bucket. I noticed his shaggy hair and beard and his travel-stained clothes—obviously fresh from the trail, just like us. I wondered what he used to do for a living, back before everything changed. Funny to think—he could have been a banker or accountant or a cell-phone salesman. Now, it seemed the trek had been the great equalizer. Everyone looked scruffy and tired. Everyone had the same little house, the same tin bucket.

"Get used to this," Mom said to Jarron, handing him the bucket. "Looks like we'll be doing this pretty often." We left him in line and went back into our house.

Mom knelt on the floor, and Dad, Ethan, and I sat down beside her.

"Before we look inside this sack, let's pray." We all bowed our heads. Mom sobbed her way through a prayer of gratitude, and instead of getting annoyed, I cried along with her.

She opened the sack (now I saw it had a 5 written on the side with marker, presumably to show it was meant for a five-person family) and pulled out plastic bags of flour, sugar, salt, yeast, and oil. Next came little packets of dried beans, then oatmeal, then powdered milk, then five small white potatoes. Then she opened a paper-wrapped bundle which held about a pound of some kind of meat. There were matches, soap, and candles nestled inside a small cooking pot, which was in good shape but obviously not new. Lastly, she pulled out five bowls, spoons, and cups, one paring knife, and a piece of paper.

"Dear Members," Mom read. "Welcome to Missouri and your new home. Please accept this starter package with our love. Many people labored to prepare it for you. Starting tomorrow, you will be able to redeem your remaining credits for other things of your choice at the bishop's storehouse such as wood; cloth for towels, bedding, and clothing; kitchen tools, and other food items. Over time, many other goods will become available, such as furniture and other things for your home. It will be your choice how you spend—or save—your credits. Don't worry about tithing. We're living a higher law now.

"You will have the privilege of working to earn more credits and to build our city. Starting tomorrow, you may come to the churchyard, where you'll be given a choice of several assignments. All are of equal importance. You will also have an assignment in your ward given to you by your bishop in the next few weeks.

"Thank you for your faith and strength. We look forward to working beside you to build the kingdom. Signed, Your Stake Presidency."

I felt a little hum of excitement. What would my assignment be?

Jarron walked in with the bucket of water. "Perfect timing," Mom said. She surveyed the food items. "Okay. We need to make this last at least a day or two, and it's going to take some work to turn this stuff into food. Ethan, look out back for the wood. A fire's first."

We scurried to light a fire in the stove (thank goodness for Boy Scout brothers), and soon Mom had beans cooking in the little pot, which sat directly on the flat top of the stove. Lacking a mixing bowl, she put a little salt and yeast right into the plastic bag of flour, mooshed it with her hands, and using one of the drinking cups, scooped in enough water to make a stiff dough, kneading it while still in the bag. Then she poured a little oil on top of the stove, beside the bean pot, and fried pieces of the dough in it. She put them, piping hot, into our hands. We alternated blowing on them and nibbling them. The fry bread was chewy and plain, but I thought it tasted like the best bread I'd ever eaten. We each ate two, and she continued frying until she'd used up the dough and had a nice little pile to eat later.

"Mom, super idea on the fry bread. I wonder if other people will think of it." I said.

She smiled. "I think I'll walk around to a few houses and help. In the meantime, try this." She handed me the paring knife and waved at the potatoes.

I thought maybe I'd just scrub them—peels are good for you, right? But the potatoes were pretty caked with dirt, and I had no scrubber thing. After making a muddy mess, I gave in and peeled them. The easiest things seemed difficult without all our little comforts. How much we'd taken for granted—a simple working surface, a cutting board, a stream of water at the lift of a lever.

Mom came back beaming. There'd been quite a few people who'd been stumped by the bag of ingredients. I was happy for her. Maybe here she'd have a chance to shine instead of being offbeat and eccentric. She was already famous for helping with births. Now other hippy skills were coming in handy.

The potatoes and meat went into the pot, and by evening we had a decent stew to eat with the fry bread. And just as on the trek, there wasn't much to do after dark except go to bed. Although having my own room was nice, the heat from the stove was nicer. We'd slept next to each other for months, and although the time would come for bedrooms, sheets, and pillows, we laid down on the floor by the stove and went to sleep. Our first day in Missouri was complete.

+

The next night, Zack came over.

"Finally found you!" he said. We hugged, and he hugged the rest of the family too. At last I got to see him in his Legion uniform, and of course, he looked ridiculously good in it. He looked grown-up, strong, capable—maybe it was his broad shoulders, maybe it was just the way he carried himself. He folded his arms across his chest and grinned at me. I pretty much melted.

"Where are you living?" I managed to ask.

"There's a barracks for the Legion over near the temple complex." He took my mittened hand, and we went outside to walk down the dirt street of our new neighborhood. The forty-degree weather felt balmy.

I thought about the first time we'd held hands—on the first trek, somewhere in Oregon. That seemed like about a hundred years ago. So much had changed. Zack had gone from a high school farm kid who hadn't really thought through his beliefs to a young man who'd seen death and hardship, becoming a leader full of faith and courage. I must have changed too, but how? I'd been a leader in my own way, I supposed, with my project and so on, but in some ways I felt like the same old Amélie, complete with bum leg and self-doubt coming out my ears.

Ironic that now we both limped a bit—Zack's ankle still bothered him. We made quite a pair.

He told me about his journey from Utah, with all its adventure and amazingness and miraculousness. I started to get sort of down about how mine, on the other hand, had been just plain hard. But I stopped myself. Now I knew. I knew that I—and the whole main company—had been brought through that challenge to refine us, to strengthen us for what was to come. Apparently, what was to come was huge. We'd be needing that strength.

You've come so far, I reminded myself. *You're not the same girl that used to fall into sulks for days, iPod headphones blocking out the world. You're a grown-up now. And despite all this marvelous maturity, sometimes grown-ups still have valleys to climb out of.*

"So do you know what you'll be doing for your work assignment?" Zack's voice brought me back out of reverie.

"Um, yes—they are having me help plan and schedule the youth assignments. So my assignment is to make assignments, ha ha. I'm sort of scared."

"You'll be great." Zack squeezed my hand.

"Do you like being in the Legion? Do you picture yourself staying there for a while?" Walking with Zack was ever so much nicer than using my cane. He'd been my walking partner so many times now that he knew exactly how to step, how to lend support without making me feel babied.

"Well, they did ask for a five-year commitment. It's okay. I don't mind the work. All we do right now is guard duty. That could change though."

"How so?"

"Rumor is, our whole land is pretty chaotic. There are factions trying to get power over each other, gangs, fighting—I've even heard that there are foreign troops on American soil, trying to take advantage of our weakness. And it's not just in the US. Or, I should say, what used to be the US. They say our city is the only place on the whole earth that's peaceful."

That set me back. "How can that be? We just walked through miles and miles of country and never saw that kind of stuff. We didn't see much of anything at all."

"Well, you're right about that—empty spaces exist—but the cities are either bombed out, in chaos, or under attack, either from factions or foreigners."

I shivered. What was happening back in Salt Lake City? What was happening in Washington State, my old home?

Would I live here in Missouri for the rest of my life? I never imagined that in all my growing up years. This was New Jerusalem, and everything was crazy amazing, but I still felt a flicker of sad nostalgia for my home in Zillah.

"And there's something else that's going to change about my assignment. I've been sort of dreading telling you this."

My heart hit the ground. Now what?

He continued. "They're sending me to patrol an area on the other side of Jackson County for the next three months. The Church has a ranch there, plus some grain storage. Like I was saying, if and when things heat up, my assignment would probably change. I could be pulled back here or even sent somewhere farther away. But for now, I'm supposed to head out to the ranch in a week."

I knew it. I knew this couldn't last. As we'd walked, I'd already plotted how we'd do this every night. I'd have Zack each evening all to myself. If he got posted out there, I'd hardly ever see him. No way every night. We'd be lucky to see each other once a month.

I tried not to cry. Oh, how I tried. Still, tears leaked from the corners of my eyes and coursed down my cheeks. At least I didn't sob out loud, which would be so embarrassing.

A realization came over me, one that seemed a bit strange but made sense at the same time. The love I felt for Zack had grown and deepened because of faith—faith that we'd see each other again, yes, but also because our faith in God had grown through our experiences, and that common bond drew us closer.

Love deepened by faith.

And now he'd be going away again. I guessed I'd have to keep having faith that somehow we'd be able to be together the way I yearned for.

Faith deepened by love.

We came upon a dark, empty church building, and Zack drew me over to its steps. We sat down, and he put his arm around me, his eyes staring out into the night sky, which was studded with a million stars.

"You know, the Legion does have a policy that exempts certain soldiers from this kind of posting," he said, his voice quiet and solemn.

"Oh, really? What is it?"

"Married soldiers are being posted here in the city. They're exempt from being sent out on these faraway postings, at least for now."

His words fell over me in a prickling shower. I couldn't speak. He turned his face toward me, and our eyes locked.

"I know we're young," he said. "So young. Nineteen." He crinkled his nose in that way I adored. "Like people were in the old days when they got married."

I drew a shaky breath. Two breaths.

"Amélie, say something," he whispered.

"Do you remember when we talked about this the very first time, sitting by the reflecting pool at the temple?"

"Yes." Zack smiled, and pink bloomed on his cheeks.

"We're young now, but back then—good grief—we were babies."

He laughed. "That was less than a year ago."

"I don't know why, but I feel so much older now. Way older."

"We've been through a lot." He paused. "When you say you feel older, what do you mean? Do you mean that maybe we're old enough to think about this?"

"We are thinking about this, whether we're old enough or not."

"Lee, I think we're supposed to be together. You feel that way too, right?"

I nodded.

"Sooner or later, I hope we get married. Maybe we should do it sooner. There's hard times coming. Wouldn't it be easier if we were facing them together? I could stay around. You know, look after you."

I smiled. Only Zack could say "look after you" without getting my hackles up. "Zack, are you trying to convince me to get married using logic?"

"I guess so." He looked sheepish.

"I don't care how *logical* it is to get married. All I know is I feel like doing it no matter how ridiculous it is."

"You do?" He grinned.

"Don't bother trying to act surprised."

"Well, I am, a little. The part about it being now, that is. Wait, wait . . . hang on." He slid his arm from around my back and then knelt on one knee in front of me.

He pulled in a deep breath. "Amélie Hatch, will you marry me? This week? In whatever temple we can find that's finished enough to perform sealings? Because it seems the end of the world is coming, and I love you."

I put my arms around his neck. "Yes, Zack Allman, I will marry you this very week. Because I love you. But even though it seems like the world is covered in darkness—and it's going to get even darker—it's not the end of the world. It's the beginning. The beginning of us together, but more than that. Light will come—first only a glimmering. Then so, so much light everywhere. And it will never be dark again."

ABOUT THE AUTHOR

MARGOT HOVLEY WAS RAISED IN rural Washington State, where she worked as a girl pig herder and champion produce box–maker. She now lives and plays in Utah with her big family. When she's not storytelling, she's hanging out with family, teaching music to the somewhat-willing, and playing sports. She loves hiking, traveling, and concocting adventures.